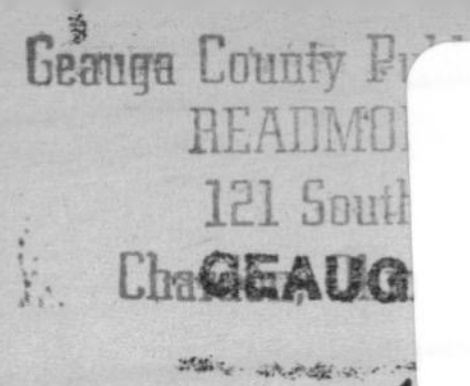

RENEGADE'S REVENGE

Tom Ludlow lifted Smith's arm and felt for a pulse. Nothing. The man was dead, but the body was still warm.

Suddenly the thought hit Ludlow that Fargo might be here now. It paralyzed him even before he heard a floor board squeak behind him. He knew he should pull his gun and whirl; he might get in a lucky shot. But fear froze him there in the middle of the room. He sat huddled beside Smith's body, unable to move.

Then the roof fell on him and he toppled forward on his face. He did not hear the wall clock strike ten o'clock.

WAYNE D. OVERHOLSER

Twice Winner of the Spur Award and Winner of the Lifetime Achievement Award from the Western Writers of America

Other *Leisure Books* by Wayne D. Overholser:

WAYNE D. OVERHOLSER

THE JUDAS GUN

LEISURE BOOKS NEW YORK CITY

A LEISURE BOOK®

March 1992

This edition is reprinted by arrangement with MACMILLAN PUBLISHING COMPANY, a division of Macmillan, Inc.

Dorchester Publishing Co., Inc.
276 Fifth Avenue
New York, NY 10001

For further information, contact: Macmillan Publishing Co., a division of Macmillan Inc., 866 Third Avenue, New York, NY 10022

Printed in the United States of America.

THE JUDAS GUN

One

Shorty Bogardus left his house on the east edge of San Lorenzo at exactly 4:55 A.M. By walking briskly he could reach his livery stable in five minutes. Not that there was any logical reason for him to operate by the clock. It was simply a matter of habit.

On the other hand, there was no reason to lie in bed, either. He was a widower—he had lost his wife a year ago—and it was loneliness as much as anything that drove him out of his house at the same hour every morning.

He strode past the bank and the San Lorenzo House toward his livery stable directly ahead. He had thought some of getting married again, but at his age, he was sixty, the chance of finding a woman he wanted stood at zero.

Still, age didn't stop some men. Take old Judge Wallace in his fine house on the hill north of town. Over seventy, the Judge was, and on his third wife. He'd been out looking while his second lay on her deathbed. Before she was gone six months, he'd married a seventeen-year-old girl.

But Shorty wasn't Judge Wallace. If he had the Judge's money, he could . . .

Shorty stopped in front of his livery stable, one hand out-stretched. He stood motionless a good thirty seconds, as if the chill spring morning had frozen him in that position. Even in the pale gray light he could see the words that someone had chalked across the door: FARGO IS COMING.

He dropped his hand to his side. Fear crawled into his belly and tied a knot in his insides. His leg muscles twitched, his heart began to pound, and for a moment he was unable to catch a good, deep breath.

The last thing Shorty Bogardus wanted was for Ben Fargo to come back. Two years ago he'd been tried and convicted for stealing a calf, and Judge Wallace had thrown the book at him. He must have broken out of the pen at Canon City. The Judge had sentenced him to ten years.

Shorty would never forget what had happened after the Judge pronounced sentence. Before Sheriff Tom Ludlow could stop him, Fargo yelled that no pen in the world could hold him. He'd come back and kill the son of a bitchin' Judge and every bastard who was on the jury. Even if he was guilty, which he wasn't, what kind of justice was it to give a man ten years for stealing a three-months-old calf?

Ludlow dragged him out of the courthouse and down the stairs to the jail, Fargo yelling and cursing hysterically. There wasn't a man in the courthouse, especially the eleven who sat in the jury box with Shorty, who didn't believe Fargo would try to do exactly what he threatened. Shorty hadn't had the slightest doubt, and he didn't now. Fargo was known to have killed at least three men for far less reason than he had to kill Judge Wallace and twelve jurymen.

Now, staring at the words on the stable door, Shorty

wondered if he'd be the first man Fargo would try to kill. No, he'd go after Wallace first. Shorty's immediate thought was that he ought to warn the Judge, but Wallace wouldn't be awake yet. Anyhow, this was a job for the sheriff.

Forcing his rubbery knees to hold him upright, Shorty started to run. Tom Ludlow was a bachelor who lived only a block north of the stable between Main Street and the Judge's mansion on the hill, but it was the longest block Shorty had ever run. He staggered up the path and pounded on Ludlow's front door. When he couldn't raise anyone, he went around to the back and pounded again. Still no answer.

Shorty leaned against the wall, breathing hard. He looked across the vacant lot to Marge Rainer's house, a small, neat cottage painted white with green trim. Marge was a widow who had moved to town three years ago when her rancher husband had died.

The story was around that she wasn't straight, that Ludlow was living with her. Shorty didn't believe it. He liked and respected her, so he'd put the story down as an ugly chunk of gossip coming from the old women of San Lorenzo. It was true that Ludlow had been seen coming out of her house at odd hours, but that didn't prove she let him get into bed with her.

Shorty remained on Ludlow's porch until he had his wind back. He had a terrible fear that the sheriff was over there with Marge, but he couldn't force himself to go to her house and find out. Anyhow, the man to see was the deputy, Clint Harper. Ludlow was a bag of wind. Clint always took care of the dangerous jobs. Shorty guessed that was the reason Ludlow had hired Clint in the first place.

Shorty started running again, this time toward the courthouse which was at the other end of Main Street. He remembered that the jailer was sick and Clint was sleeping in the sheriff's office instead of his room in the San Lorenzo House.

He wasn't sure what he'd do if he learned that the gossip about Marge was true. He didn't like the idea of Ludlow taking advantage of her. The man just wasn't any good. Chances were he'd make her a lot of fancy promises, but he'd never marry her.

Fact was, Ludlow wasn't a fit man for sheriff. He wouldn't have been elected in the first place if Judge Wallace hadn't given him a pat on the back, and in San Lorenzo County getting a pat on the back from Wallace was enough to elect a yellow dog. Shorty often wondered what Ludlow would do if he didn't have a solid man like Clint Harper for a deputy. He'd be in a sad fix, that was sure.

When Shorty reached the courthouse, he found Clint asleep on a cot in the sheriff's office. He grabbed the deputy by the shoulder and shook him awake, shouting, "Get up, Clint. Get up. I've got something to show you."

Clint grunted and turned over. "It ain't daylight yet. It's too early to get up."

"Come on," Shorty shouted. "I'll get me a bucket of water and throw it on you if you don't get out of bed."

Clint sat up and rubbed his eyes. "What time is it? I feel like I just went to bed."

"It's after five," Shorty snapped. "Come on, damn it. If the courthouse was burning down, you'd go with it."

Clint yawned, got into his pants, and then pulled on his boots. "I don't smell any smoke," he said, and yawned again.

"You ain't moving fast enough to make any," Shorty said.

Clint crossed the room, poured water from a bucket into a tin basin, and washed. He ran a comb through his heavy brown hair, and yawned a third time. He returned to the cot, strapped his gun belt around him, and picking up his Stetson, said, "Sometimes I think there's a plot on foot to keep me from sleeping. This had better be good."

"It's good enough," Shorty said grimly. "Or bad enough is a better way of saying it."

They went along the hall and down the steps. Shorty had to run to keep up with Clint, who stood six feet two without his boots, a full head taller than Shorty. By the time they reached the street, Shorty had the feeling he'd been running all morning. He'd be stove up the rest of the day.

"Want to tell me what's biting you?" Clint asked.

"You'll find out, and you won't like it no better'n me." Shorty was silent until they were opposite Sam Calloway's store, until he couldn't stand it any longer. He said, "I went to get Ludlow, but he wasn't home. You got any idea where he'd be this time of morning?"

Clint glanced at him sharply, then shrugged his shoulders. "Hard to tell. He's a sound sleeper."

"He couldn't have slept through my pounding," Shorty said. "I hammered on his back door and front one, too, and I couldn't raise him. Naw, he wasn't at home." When Clint remained silent, Shorty asked, "You think maybe he's over at Marge's?"

"Might be. He eats breakfast with her sometimes."

"Wasn't no smoke coming out of her chimney," Shorty said. "I looked. You think maybe he was over there sleeping with her?"

"You've been listening to the old women talk," Clint said. "I'm surprised at you."

They reached the front of the stable, and Shorty pointed to the words on the door. Clint swung around to face him. "You mean you got me out of bed just to show me that?"

"That's exactly what I done," Shorty said. "You wasn't on that jury. I was. You wasn't a deputy then, but you know Fargo."

"I know him, all right," Clint said. "I went to school

with him. But hell, man, this is just some kid stunt. You sure it wasn't there last night?"

"I'm sure," Shorty said, "and I don't figure it's any kid stunt. He's got some friend here in town who wants to get us good and scared before he shows up. That's what we'll be, too. You'd better let the Judge know. He'd be the first one Fargo would go after."

Clint scratched the back of his neck thoughtfully. "I don't know how smart it is to get everybody in town worked up over something we don't know means anything. Fargo was sent up for ten years. No way he could be coming back unless he broke out, and we'd have heard about it if that had happened."

"How?" Shorty demanded. "The wires between here and Grand Junction have been down for two, three days. Chances are there hasn't been time to get word by mail, coming twice a week like it does."

"That's right," Clint agreed, "but it still leaves us right where we were. No way we can find out for sure."

"After he gets here and kills half a dozen people, you'll be sure. You gonna wait for that?"

"No. Guess I'd better drop it in Ludlow's lap."

"Where you gonna look for him?"

"Oh, I'll turn him up somewhere," Clint said carelessly. "You go ahead and open up."

Shorty watched him walk away and turn north toward the sheriff's house. But Marge's house was in that direction, too. That's where he is, Shorty thought. That sure as hell is where he is.

Two

AS A MATTER OF POLICY, CLINT KNOCKED ON LUDLOW'S front and back doors. No answer. Clint had been reasonably sure there wouldn't be after hearing that Shorty had been here a few minutes before. Ludlow was a fool, or he'd leave Marge's house before daylight. But the sheriff was a lazy man who never got out of bed any sooner than he had to. By staying over there, he'd get Marge to cook breakfast for him.

Clint hesitated, knowing that Ludlow would be sore if Clint caught him in Marge's house, but Ludlow had to know about the message on the livery stable door. Besides, he needed a jolt. So did Marge. There was no sense making what they were doing public knowledge.

Clint crossed the vacant lot between the two houses, and noticed that smoke was beginning to drift from the chimney of Marge's kitchen. He stepped up on the back porch, knocked, and when no one answered knocked again. This time steps sounded across the kitchen floor.

Marge opened the back door, looked at him, and said in surprise, "Why, good morning, Clint. Isn't this pretty early for you to be out?"

She was a good-looking woman with a gentle manner and a kind face, one who did not deserve to be hurt. And she would be. Clint was sure of that, knowing Ludlow as well as he did. He had often wondered how the sheriff could do some of the things he did, but Clint didn't consider it his business to talk to the man about his morals.

"Good morning, Marge," Clint said. "I apologize for calling at this time of day, but I've got to see Tom."

She backed up a step and put her hand to her throat. She was wearing a maroon robe over her nightgown, and her chestnut hair hung down her back. She had a lock of white hair directly above her right eye which, in Clint's opinion, made her look distinguished. She was a little on the plump side, but not too much so. It was the kind of figure that many men found attractive, although Clint's personal taste ran more to slender women.

"I don't know anything about Tom," Marge said. "Maybe he's home."

"Let's not waste time talking about where Tom isn't." Stepping inside, Clint closed the door. "You'll never get your kitchen warmed up this way."

Marge backed up another step, saying plaintively, "Clint, I don't know much about law, but unless you've got a search warrant . . ."

"Why, you know how Tom operates," Clint said. "He just pulls his gun and says it's all the search warrant he needs."

He walked past her into the front room and turned toward the bedroom. Ludlow was asleep, his back to the door. Clint said loudly, "Good morning, Tom."

Ludlow reared up in bed as suddenly as if someone had rammed a pin into him. He let out a shrill yell and dived off the bed for his gun, which lay in a holster on the floor.

Clint took one step forward and kicked it across the room.

"You ought to be sure you're shooting an enemy, not a friend," Clint admonished.

Ludlow sat on the edge of the bed and rubbed his eyes. "I don't know how much of a friend you are," he grumbled. "I ought to shoot you on general principles." He wiped a hand across his face, thoroughly angry now that he was awake. "What the hell right have you got to come in here? You're a fool. What's more, you're fired."

Clint shrugged and started to remove the star from his vest. "All right, Tom. I guess I am a fool, drawing half the money you do and taking all the risks. I've been thinking of running against you this fall, and I couldn't do that while I was your deputy."

"All right!" Ludlow's face turned red. "You ain't fired. Leave that star where it is. But I still say you're a fool, busting in here like this."

"You're the fool," Clint said, thoroughly irritated. "It happens that I like Marge. A lot of men in this town do, but you're the only one who gets into bed with her. I don't reckon any of us want to give her a worse name than she's got now, and it sure ain't good, the way the town women talk about her. If you had a teaspoonful of brains, you'd be out of here before daylight."

Clint turned and strode out of the bedroom. He didn't like Ludlow. He didn't even respect him. No one did unless it was Marge and Judge Wallace, and the reason Wallace liked him was because Ludlow carried out his orders. But at that Clint doubted if the Judge respected Ludlow. The old man was funny that way. He was more inclined to respect the men who fought him.

Clint went into the kitchen and sat down at the table. He rolled a cigarette, watching Marge who stood at the stove with her back to him. Without looking around, she said, "Stay for breakfast, Clint."

"Glad to," he said. "I guess it'll be better for your

reputation if me and Tom leave together. That is, if you're interested in keeping what's left of your reputation."

She turned to him and he saw that she had been crying. "Of course I am," she said. "What are people saying?"

"The women think the worst and the men think the best," he said. "You're a man's woman, Marge. I've got a hunch that's the way you want it."

"It's the way it's always been," she said sadly, "but not the way I want it." She turned back to the bacon she was frying.

When Marge's husband had been alive, they had lived on the ranch just east of Clint's. That had been in the good days when Clint had owned the Rafter C and had been full of dreams about the great outfit he'd own someday, dreams that had turned into a giant-size nightmare when the bank had taken his spread away from him.

He'd been young, engaged to marry Nan Carney, and he was working his tail off to make a go of it when the bank cleaned him out. It should have carried him another year, and he wasn't sure to this day whether it had been Judge Wallace or Doug Carney, who ran the bank for the Judge, who was responsible for the foreclosure.

Carney was Nan's father and had never favored Clint for a son-in-law, so Clint suspected Carney was the one. Wallace could have stopped it, but it wasn't his way to turn down a good small spread when it could be had for a song.

Clint finished his cigarette and, walking to the stove, lifted a lid and tossed the stub inside. Marge asked, "When are you and Nan getting married?"

"When Nan and me have enough saved to start over," he said. "One thing's sure. We won't get married as long as I'm packing this star."

"I'll loan you the money to buy a spread," she said. "You can run it on shares or pay the loan back when you can. Any way you want it."

"Thank you kindly and I'll turn it down again," he said. "No sense of you getting into trouble with the Judge, and that's right where it would put you."

She fished the bacon out of the frying pan, silent now. He stood beside her, looking at her, thinking how perfectly mated she and her husband had been. They had worked together day after day, and Marge was capable of doing almost anything a man could do. Clint, living beside them, had been their best friend and they had been his.

When Vince Rainer died suddenly, Clint helped Marge sell her ranch and find a house in town. Now he wished he'd tried to get her to leave the country, but it had never occurred to him that she would get involved with Tom Ludlow.

He watched her break half a dozen eggs into the frying pan. She went to the door of the front room and called, "Breakfast in a couple of minutes, Tom," and returned to the stove.

Clint said, "Marge, you can tell me it's none of my business, but I'm going to say it anyway. Break it off with Tom. He'll never marry you."

She glanced at him miserably and said, "It's been lonely since I moved to town. I haven't had any friends among the women except Nan and Bonita Wallace who's as sad as I am. So I was glad to have Tom's company at first. Then it got out of hand before I knew it."

"You know now," Clint said. "Break it off while you can."

"Clint," she said, "did it ever occur to you that I'd rather have a little than nothing? I had Vince for so long. Now I don't think I could live without a little love."

Ludlow came in, a hand brushing at his curly black hair that he wore long. He was proud of his hair and sweeping mustache, and of his clothes, black from his Stetson to his expensive boots, their somber tone relieved only by the star on his vest, the silver-plated belt buckle, and the pearl-handled revolver in the holster.

Handsome by some standards, Clint thought, but not by mine. Ludlow was all bluff, and there would come a day when something would happen which would show the whole county exactly what he was. Alongside the man Vince Rainer had been, Ludlow was no more than a thin shadow. Marge must be aware of that, but Clint guessed it was the way she'd said, that she'd rather have a little than nothing.

"You ready to talk yet?" Ludlow demanded as he crossed the kitchen to the sink and pumped a basin of water.

He was still surly, so Clint waited until Ludlow washed and carefully combed his hair, thinking that his dislike for the man had grown so during the year he'd worn the deputy's star that now he was seriously considering resigning.

Clint would have quit before this if he could have found another job that paid as well. He saved a few dollars every month, and Nan, who taught the lower grades, was saving too. Still, it would be a long time before they had enough in the bank to warrant seriously looking for a ranch.

When Ludlow turned from the mirror on the wall, Clint said, "Shorty Bogardus got me out of bed a little after five and took me to the livery stable. Someone had written across the front of the door in chalk. Shorty swears there wasn't any writing there last night."

"Well?" Ludlow demanded. "What was it?"

"Fargo is coming," Clint said. "That's all. Just three words."

Those three words were enough to take the color out of Ludlow's face. He staggered to the table and sat down. He rubbed his forehead and then blurted, "Hell, Clint. It's just a fool trick that somebody's played figuring to tree the town."

"I thought of that," Clint said. "It's what I told Shorty at first, but now I don't think so. It'll tree the town, all right, but it's my guess there's a reason. Fargo's the kind who'd want everybody scared before he showed. He's probably laughing his head off just thinking about it."

"But it ain't time for him to be let out."

Clint shrugged. "All right, he broke out. I know him, Tom. Better'n you do. We're the same age. We were in the same grade for several years and we had a fight on an average of once a week. Now I don't claim I know exactly how he thinks, but I can sure guess. He'll wait until he figures the whole town is so boogered we're ready to tuck our tails and run, then he'll show up. He'll kill the Judge and maybe Doug Carney because he was foreman of the jury. Maybe he'll get you because you were pretty rough on him when you had him in jail. He'll clean the bank out. Maybe the safe in Calloway's store and shoot Sam, since he was on the jury. Then he'll clear out for the Utah line. He's got nothing to lose. Remember that, Tom."

Marge had placed the platter of eggs and bacon on the table and poured the coffee. "Eat your breakfast before it gets cold," she said.

Clint obeyed, but Ludlow didn't seem hungry. He was silent a good three minutes, then he demanded, "You telling me he'll do this all by himself?"

"No," Clint said. "I can't make a guess who'll be with him, but we know one thing: He's got a friend in town. The man who did the writing. If he broke out of the pen, he didn't do it alone. And another thing: Everybody thought he used to ride with a bunch of ridge runners from the other side of the line. Maybe they're waiting for him to show up and then they'll hit town. Or he might be with them now."

"As I remember it," Marge said, "he swore he'd kill every man who was on the jury. They should be warned, the ones that are still around."

Clint nodded. "That's right. He's the kind who never forgets anything. A couple of years in the pen won't change him."

Ludlow pushed his plate back. "Got any idea what we should do?"

"We've got to tell the Judge," Clint said. "Another thing that keeps buzzing in my head is how did this someone who did the writing know that Fargo broke out? It's a good guess that a telegram came in before the wire was cut. I'd like to see the telegrams that have come in the last four, five days."

Ludlow rose. "I'll go see what they were. You tell the Judge."

"Now hold on," Clint said angrily. "The Judge will raise Cain if you don't tell him."

"Do what I say," Ludlow said, and, picking up his Stetson, left the kitchen.

"Thanks for the breakfast, Marge," Clint said, and ran after Ludlow, catching up in time to go through the front door together.

When they reached the street, Clint said, "Tom, I've got something to tell you and you'd better listen."

Ludlow swung around to face him. "Well, I'm listening."

"I like Marge too much to see her get hurt. Marry her or quit seeing her."

Ludlow got red in the face. He blew out a great breath, and shouted, "Ain't you getting out of line, telling me what to do?"

"Not with Marge. You're the one who got out of line. If you get her into trouble and don't marry her, I'll take a knife to you. That's a promise."

Ludlow swore, glared at Clint, then wheeled and strode away. Clint watched him a moment, not sure he had listened. He turned toward Judge Wallace's house, glancing at his watch as he started up the hill. It was then six-thirty.

THREE

JUDGE WALLACE HAD LIVED IN THREE HOUSES SINCE HE'D come to San Lorenzo nearly twenty years ago. Then it had been only a tiny frontier settlement; the Utes had been moved off the reservation just a few months before Wallace arrived. Clint was a small boy when his folks moved to San Lorenzo, but he remembered exactly how the town had looked, and he remembered Judge Wallace.

At that time Wallace had been a middle-aged lawyer who apparently didn't have two silver dollars to jingle in his pocket. Clint had never heard anything about the Judge's background. He might have been an outright failure through those early years, or the hard times of the seventies might have wiped him out. Possibly he had never met up with the right opportunities until he came to San Lorenzo.

Wallace had grown with the town and the surrounding range country, a vast, nearly level plateau which lay between the San Lorenzo River on the north, the Cloud

Mountains to the east, and the Dolores River to the west.

To the south the grassland gave way to a maze of canyons and slickrock rims, an area so rough and arid it was almost useless. It was here that Ben Fargo had his ranch that was supposed to have been a hideout for the Wild Bunch with which he rode.

Today the plateau was known as Wallace Mesa, a fitting enough name, since the Judge owned or controlled practically everything on it. Clint thought about that as he paused on the crest of the hill and looked down at the town, just now coming to life with pillars of smoke rising from nearly every chimney into the clear, sun-bright air. Whether people liked it or not, the fact remained that Judge Ezra Wallace had a strangle hold on nearly every business in San Lorenzo.

Wallace had built his first house on the east edge of town, the house where Shorty Bogardus lived now. His wife had been a small, pert woman who knew how to handle him. She might have been his conscience. Clint often wondered about it. In any case, she died soon after they arrived in San Lorenzo. Shortly thereafter Wallace married his second wife, an easy-going, colorless woman, and he was on his way.

Wallace had built his second house three years later on the slope directly below where Clint stood, the house in which the storekeeper, Sam Calloway, lived now.

Clint could not put his finger on precisely what Wallace had done to achieve success. It had been so gradual at first. His law practice gave him a little money, then he'd bought several lots on Main Street, and later he put up business buildings which he rented. After that he bought a controlling interest in the bank.

Next he established a stage line between San Lorenzo and Grand Junction, and soon he was operating a freight service that hauled nearly everything that came to San Lorenzo. He'd wound up with the toll bridge which spanned the San Lorenzo River just above its junction with the Dolores.

His last venture had been the purchase of the Box W north of town, the biggest and most prosperous spread on the mesa. He had not lost his Midas touch, for the Box W prospered as everything else had which he owned. All this time his political power had grown until he not only controlled San Lorenzo County, but the four neighboring counties as well.

Turning, Clint walked on up the path to the front door. Wallace had built this house four years ago, a mansion that was completely out of place in San Lorenzo. His wife had died the following winter, and he had married Bonita Ivor soon afterward.

Clint yanked the bell pull, wondering about this marriage as he wondered about many things that concerned Ezra Wallace. A man's luck was bound to run out sometime, and when a seventy-year-old man marries an attractive girl, he is giving disaster an invitation, especially if the girl was a flirt like Bonita.

She opened the door and smiled when she saw who it was. "Come in, Mr. Harper," she said. "I was just getting breakfast for the Judge. Come on back to the kitchen and you can eat with me. The Judge takes his breakfast in bed."

"Thanks," he said, "but I just had breakfast with Marge and Tom Ludlow."

"Well, you can still drink a cup of coffee with me," she said as she closed the door behind him.

Bonita wore a pink-and-white checked housedress that made a snug fit over her hips. She had a way of walking with a switching movement that invariably fired a man's blood, and Clint was convinced that she was fully aware of the effect she had. But he did not suspect her of being unfaithful. She wouldn't be foolish enough to risk losing the Judge's fortune by having an affair with a man nearer her own age, however much she might desire it.

She motioned to a chair at the kitchen table. "Sit down. I'll pour you a cup of coffee, then I'll take the Judge's breakfast to him. He's so stove up with rheumatism that he seldom gets out of bed."

She brought a cup and the coffeepot to the table, bent over him so that a breast touched his shoulder, and poured the coffee. "If you'll excuse me, I'll fix the Judge's mush. Then I'll have a cup of coffee with you as soon as I take his tray to him."

She was a dark girl with black eyes and brown hair. Her mother must have been Mexican, or part Indian. Her skin was a trifle swarthy, but did not detract from her beauty. Her lips were full and red, and smiled easily. Clint had not been this close to her for some time, and now as she turned slowly from him, he had the feeling that her smile was a little forced. There were crow's feet around her eyes that he had not noticed before, too many for a girl her age.

"Tell the Judge I want to see him," Clint said. "Right away. I've got something important to tell him."

She nodded as she spooned oatmeal mush into a bowl and poured the coffee. Picking up the tray, she said, "You mean you didn't come to see me?"

"I'll have to admit it was business with the Judge that brought me here," he said.

"I was afraid that was the case when I saw who was at the door." She pouted a moment, then smiled again. "But I should be used to it. No one ever comes to see me except Marge. I don't know what we'd do without each other."

She left then, and Clint drank his coffee, thinking that Bonita probably came in for as much gossip as Marge. Judge Wallace could control almost everything but the tongues of the San Lorenzo women.

Bonita returned a moment later. "He'll see you now," she said.

He rose and followed her along the hall and up the stairs, thinking how much this was like the feudal times when the lord of the manor graciously and condescendingly sent word that he'd see one of his swordsmen. In those days it probably did not arouse resentment, but it didn't work in San Lorenzo. Wallace's ego had grown with his fortune. He had become particularly obnoxious in the four years since he had moved into this house, and it was during these same four years that his neighbors' hatred had grown to its present virulence.

Wallace was sitting up in bed, a red shawl thrown over his shoulders. At one time he had been a strong and vigorous man, but he'd turned flabby, and age and rheumatism had kept him inside the house most of the winter. His jowls hung loosely at the side of his face; he was bald except for a fringe of white hair, and in the last few months his skin had taken on the appearance of gray crepe.

When Clint stepped into the bedroom, Wallace was greedily spooning mush into his mouth, now and then stopping to wipe the sleeve of his nightgown across his white mustache. He glanced up briefly, said, "Morning, Harper," and went on eating.

"Morning, Judge," Clint said, and stood just inside the door, staring at Wallace.

Merely looking at the man was enough to arouse a sickening fury in Clint. He thought about the ranch he had lost, about Nan and how they would have been married by now if he'd been given any kind of chance, and he couldn't keep from demanding, "You still claim it was Doug Carney who was responsible for stealing my outfit?"

Wallace stopped eating and looked up, a dribble of cream running down his chin. "Well, by God, is that what you came up here to ask me at this time of morning?"

"No, but I'm here and I'm asking."

"All right, I'll answer you once more. Don't ask me again. It was Carney. Now what do you want?"

Clint bit his lower lip and glanced at Bonita, who seemed amused by the fact that she was not the only one who was ground down to nothing by Wallace's domineering manner.

"Tom and me thought you ought to know that when Shorty Bogardus got to his livery stable this morning, someone had written 'Fargo is coming' with chalk across his front door. It wasn't there when Shorty left yesterday evening."

Wallace was startled enough to look up from his bowl of mush. Then he grunted, "Hogwash," and continued with his breakfast.

Clint shrugged and turned to the door. The Judge had been told. If he wanted to think it was hogwash, he could think it.

"Hold on," Wallace bellowed. "Why didn't Ludlow tell me?"

"He sent me," Clint said from the doorway. "You'll have to ask him why he didn't come."

"I sure as hell will. I don't like talking to the Number Two man when the Number One should be up here."

That was gratitude for you, Clint thought as he took another step into the hall.

"Damn it, I said to hold on," Wallace shouted. "If you two think Fargo has broken out of the pen, which I doubt, I expect you to see I'm protected. Savvy?"

Clint stepped back into the room. "You'd better savvy something, Judge. You aren't the only one in the county who has reason to think Fargo will try to kill him. We have to look out for the others, too."

"Hell, man," Wallace said as if he were talking to someone a little slow in the head, "they're not important. I *am*. If you want to keep your job, you'd better see I'm protected."

''Why Judge,'' Clint said softly, ''I don't care much whether I keep my job or not. The way I see it, you can provide your own protection. What about Andy Downs? Isn't he still your yardman?''

''Yes,'' Bonita said. ''We can afford to hire Andy, but we can't afford any help in the house.''

''You're young and strong,'' Wallace snapped at her. ''You can do the housework, but you know damned well I can't do the yard work.'' He pointed a skinny finger at Clint. ''Your idea isn't worth anything. Andy's a good man with a pitchfork, but he doesn't know which end of a gun a bullet comes out of. You and Ludlow are supposed to know. One of you stays here.''

''I'll tell Tom,'' Clint said, and turned again and this time walked to the stairs.

He stood there a moment, one hand on the banister. He had not felt this kind of anger for months. Wallace always affected him in much the same way, but in the past his reaction had been mild enough so that his sane judgment had not been upset.

Now he fought a wild and crazy desire to return to the Judge's bedroom and minutely describe to him the kind of selfish, crawling thing that he was. He would have gone back if Bonita hadn't left the room. Seeing the expression on his face, she shook her head at him and touched his arm.

''Don't,'' she whispered, and going past him down the stairs, motioned for him to follow.

When he caught up with her at the front door, she looked up at him, her expression one of calculating hatred. She asked in a low tone, ''Is there anybody who loves him, or even has a kind thought about him?''

''Maybe Tom Ludlow,'' Clint said. ''Do you?''

''No,'' she said passionately. ''I hate him even more than I hate my father. Do you feel sorry for me?''

"I have felt sorry for you from the day you married the old goat," he said.

She smiled. "Come back sometime," she said, "to see me."

She swayed toward him, her full, red lips parted. She wanted to be kissed and he wanted to satisfy her, as a means of striking at Wallace if nothing else, but he could not for a moment forget that he was in love with Nan. He said, "I'll do it," and left the house.

At the crest of the hill he looked back at the big house with its mansard roof and the colored glass in the front door and the row of cottonwoods that had been planted in front. Funny, he thought, how typical it was for a man of Wallace's caliber to live up here on the hill overlooking everyone in town. It was a tangible way of showing the townspeople they were inferior to him and must take orders from him.

He walked down the hill in long, swift strides, suddenly finding it unbearable even to be up here on the hill in front of Wallace's house.

He glanced at his watch. It was five minutes after seven.

FOUR

TOM LUDLOW WAS IN THE SHERRIF'S OFFICE WHEN CLINT walked in. Clint took off his hat and slammed it against the desk. ''Next time you can take care of your own dirty chores.''

''What did he say?'' Ludlow demanded.

''He says that next time he'll talk to the Number One man, not Number Two. And he says for us to play nursemaid to him if we think Fargo has really broken out of the pen. It's up to us to protect him.''

''Why hell,'' Ludlow said, surprised. ''Does he think he's the only man in town?''

''He sure does. He said the others weren't important. I reminded him he had a yardman, but he says Andy Downs doesn't know which end of a gun the bullet comes out of.''

''He could send Andy out to Box W to bring in some of his boys,'' Ludlow said.

''And keep them from doing work he's paying them for

when one of us could do the job? Oh no, the old bastard didn't make his money that way."

Ludlow rose and walked to the window. "I wonder how much a man should be expected to take to hold a job?" he asked, as if talking to himself.

"Not as much as the Judge deals out," Clint said. "You going up there and camp till we find out about Fargo?"

"No I'm not." Ludlow spun away from the window, his handsome face bitter. "Maybe it's time the Judge was told a thing or two. Seems like he's got a lot worse this winter, bunged up like he is and not getting out of the house much. But thinking we're going up there and look out for him while Fargo has the run of the town . . ." Ludlow shook his head. "I don't guess being sheriff is that important. I've got myself to look out for, along with the jurymen who are still in the county."

Clint was surprised at even this mild show of defiance, but he then decided that it couldn't be a matter of principle or duty. As Ludlow had just admitted, he had to look out for himself. The chances were that when Fargo showed up, if he did, Ludlow would be somewhere else.

"What did you find out about the telegrams?" Clint asked.

"Oh, not much. I had to get Mickey Shawn out of bed. He says he's checked the line between here and the toll bridge and it's all right. He don't have any responsibility from the toll bridge on to Grand Junction, so he says they'll send somebody out from the other end to fix it."

"Well, they're mighty slow about it," Clint said. "This is the third day."

"That's what Mickey says. He don't understand it. He thinks it may have been fixed and gone down again. They wouldn't let it go this long."

"Were there any telegrams?"

"A few. Early Monday morning Sam Calloway ordered some barb wire. A freight outfit was leaving Grand Junction that day. The stage left Tuesday. This is Thursday. A letter mailed Monday would have come in on the stage. That's the last we could have heard from the outside. If Fargo made his break sometime Monday afternoon, there's no way we could have found out about it."

"Any wires come in?"

"A few. A couple asked about some cattle the Judge has got for sale. One was to Shorty Bogardus about a horse he wants to buy. And there was one that came in just before the line went dead. It was to Doug Carney saying Cousin Phil was coming to visit."

"Doug don't have any Cousin Phil," Clint said. "At least I never heard of him, and I think I've been around there enough to hear of every relative they've got."

"You're mighty suspicious of a man who's going to be your father-in-law," Ludlow said. "You think that telegram was some kind of code?"

"I was wondering."

The thought that Doug Carney could have anything to do with Ben Fargo breaking out of prison was too ridiculous even to consider. Clint had no reason to like Carney, who would have been jealous of any man Nan planned to marry. In Clint's case Carney had used every weapon he could lay his hands on to delay the marriage. So far he had been successful. Still, to think that the banker had anything to do with Ben Fargo's return to San Lorenzo was out of the question.

Ludlow grinned. "I'm thinking the same thing you are, Clint. Somebody in this burg is in cahoots with Fargo, but Doug Carney is the last man to suspect."

"Yeah, I guess so, but I'd still like to know who Cousin Phil is."

"We got more'n that to worry about." Ludlow sat down at his desk and, taking out a pencil and sheet of paper from a drawer, wrote for a time and then leaned back in his chair. "Give me all the names of the men you can think of who were on the jury that convicted Fargo. The ones still around, I mean."

"Well, Doug was the foreman, which is another reason he wouldn't have anything to do with Fargo. Then there was Shorty Bogardus. Sam Calloway. Bill Ivor." He paused, and added, "And Matt Smith. I think that's all."

"I forgot about Matt Smith." Ludlow wrote the name down and then added another. "Dan Tebo is dead, but Danny is around. Fargo might take it out on a ten-year-old. He's mean enough." He leaned back in his chair, eyes half closed. "Clint, this is a funny thing. Knowing that one man is coming to town is enough to booger every-one of us into holing up."

Clint pointed at the paper on Ludlow's desk. "There were twelve men on that jury. One's dead. Five are still in the county. Where are the other six?"

"Gone, because they figured Fargo would do exactly what he is doing. I'll bet every man jack of 'em is a thousand miles from here right now."

"That's why everybody in town is going to be boogered when they hear. Shorty was plenty scared this morning."

"So am I," Ludlow said. "I ain't ashamed to admit it."

"What are you going to do?"

Ludlow rubbed the back of his neck. "I dunno. Sit here and wait for him to show up, I reckon."

It was like Ludlow to sit and wait. Clint shook his head. "Bill Ivor and Matt Smith live a long ways from town, but they've got to be warned."

He walked to a map of San Lorenzo County that hung on the wall. Smith was a rancher who lived in the foothills of the Cloud Mountains east of town. He kept a small herd of cattle, but his cash crop was hay. He had the best meadows in the county, and, living on the head of Cougar Creek, he always had water. Every summer he hired a big crew of men and put up more hay than any other five ranchers on the mesa, selling most of it to Judge Wallace's Box W. He was an eccentric who lived alone except when his hay crew was with him, and it was common knowledge that he didn't trust the bank and kept his money somewhere in or around his house.

Bill Ivor, Bonita Wallace's father, lived at the toll bridge that spanned the San Lorenzo just above its junction with the Dolores. For years he had barely scraped out a living on a greasy sack spread in the broken country to the south. Then Bonita had married Wallace, and Wallace had given Bill Ivor the job at the tollgate. For the first time in the years Clint had known him, Ivor was making a decent living.

Without turning from the map, Clint said, "Want a suggestion?"

"Sure, I'll listen," Ludlow said.

"Why don't I see Doug and you tell Sam Calloway? They're the only ones in town who don't know. I'll tell Nan to keep an eye on Danny Tebo. That leaves Bill Ivor and Matt Smith."

Clint put a finger on upper Cougar Creek where Smith had his ranch. "It's about a two-hour ride to Matt's place. The tollgate is in the opposite direction, so one of us had better go see Matt and the other one tell Ivor."

He turned to face Ludlow. "It's a shorter ride to the tollgate, maybe an hour and a quarter. We can't afford to dawdle around, because when we're both gone there's no law in town. But I don't think we'll have any trouble till evening. Maybe not till tomorrow. Fargo's the kind of hairpin who would want to give folks plenty of time to worry."

Ludlow nodded. "That's what I was thinking. Besides, Fargo ain't stupid. I don't think he'll ride into town while it's daylight."

"Not if we're both alive," Clint said, "but if he knew there wasn't a law officer left in the county, he'd come on in."

"What are you driving at?"

Clint jammed his hands into his pants pockets and walked restlessly around the room. "I wish to hell we knew who wrote that note on the stable door. Somebody is playing Fargo's game. He might be playing it big enough to smoke us down. That'd make it real easy for Fargo. Who else is there that would stand up against him, especially if he rides in with a bunch of hardcases?"

Ludlow's face lost some of its color. "I hadn't thought of that. Well, I'll see Smith. You ride out to the toll bridge and tell Ivor."

Clint walked to the desk and put on his hat. It had probably occurred to Ludlow that going to the toll bridge would be the more dangerous of the two missions. If some of the outlaws who had once ridden with Fargo had holed up on the other side of the San Lorenzo River and had kept the wires out, they might be hiding close enough to the bridge to see anyone who rode in. If there was anything to Clint's idea that Fargo would want the lawmen out of the way, the outlaws wouldn't lose the chance to dry gulch whoever visited Bill Ivor.

"All right." Clint walked to the door.

Ludlow rose and said, "You'll be back in town before noon?"

Clint nodded. "I should be."

Ludlow glanced at the clock on the wall. "Half-past seven. I'll see you at the livery stable. Don't sit around and visit with Nan."

Ludlow had made no promise. Clint didn't have the slightest doubt that if the sheriff could find another man who would make a good deputy, he'd fire Clint tomorrow. Well, Clint would welcome it. He'd just about had enough of toadying to Judge Wallace and pulling Ludlow's irons out of the fire.

FIVE

KNOWING THAT NAN AND HER FATHER WOULD BE EATING breakfast this time of morning, Clint went around the house to the back door and knocked. When Nan opened the door, he asked, ''Who comes calling earlier in the morning than me?''

''You're the one man I like to have call, night or day,'' Nan said. ''Come in before the kitchen cools off.''

He stepped inside, spoke to Doug who was sitting at the table, then took Nan into his arms and kissed her. She returned his kiss, her arms encircling his neck, and then drew her head back and asked softly, ''Are we getting married today?''

''Not today,'' he said. ''I understand that things like that take planning.''

She sighed. ''So I've heard.'' She nodded at the table. ''Had breakfast?''

''With Marge and Tom Ludlow.''

"Well, you can stand a cup of my good coffee. Sit down and fight with Dad for a minute."

"It won't be hard to do that," he said.

He watched her until she disappeared into the pantry. She was a petite young woman, ninety-eight pounds of restless energy, blonde and blue-eyed, with a trim figure that made her entirely desirable in Clint's eyes. He had been in love with her since their high school days, and they had been engaged for four years. Now he was twenty-five and she was twenty-three, and marriage seemed as far off as when he'd first given the ring to her. She would marry him any time regardless of his job or the money had had in the bank, but he was cursed with a careful streak which had prevented him from letting Nan set the date.

He had seen his mother live from hand to mouth for years and become an old woman when she was forty. He would not do that to Nan, although he recognized the dismal fact that if he kept putting her off, he would lose her. By San Lorenzo standards she was an old maid; she wanted marriage and a family. He had no right to ask her to keep on waiting for him, yet he could not bear to think of giving her up.

When he sat down at the table, he glanced at Doug Carney, and the familiar bitterness welled up in him again. He would have made it with the ranch if the bank had given him one more year. Cattle prices were up. With the herd he'd owned, he could have paid the interest and part of the principal.

"I've been up to see the Judge," Clint said. "I asked him again if he was responsible for taking my ranch. I got the same answer I always get. I don't know why I keep asking it."

Carney sighed. "I don't either, Clint. You can't change what happened by harping on it all the time. What you've got to think of is the future. Times are better now. In another year the bank will back you if you want to tackle ranching again."

Nan brought Clint's coffee and sat down to finish her breakfast. Carney went on eating, more than satisfied to drop the subject. He had repeatedly told Clint that the Judge lied, that the old man knew people didn't like him, and that those who worked for him had to take the blame for his greedy acts.

If Doug Carney didn't shoulder the responsibility, he'd lose his job at the bank and Wallace would bring in a new man who would carry out his orders. That was the way Carney told it, and it was probably true, but the point was that Doug Carney was not a man to stand up for his convictions and therefore could not be trusted.

Clint had never been able to hate Carney, not because the man would someday be his father-in-law, but because he was a mild failure at anything he did, and had to be pitied. He was about fifty, a short man not much taller than Nan, with a round, pink-cheeked face and a ball of a belly which made him resemble a diminutive Santa Claus without a beard. He was always pleasant, always mild in speech and action, and seemed able to take Judge Wallace's browbeating without losing his temper.

When Nan finished her breakfast, she said, "I've got to get ready for school. Want to walk over there with me, Clint?"

"Sure do." He hesitated, hating to tell them about the writing on the livery stable door because he didn't want to worry them. But he blurted it out, adding that he and Ludlow were warning everyone who had been on the jury. "It may be just a prank, Doug," he said, "but Tom and me thought you'd better be on the lookout."

Carney had lifted his coffee cup to his lips, but he didn't drink any of it. He held the cup in front of his face, staring over it at Clint, his hand shaking so that some of the coffee dribbled over the edge. He set the cup back on the table and dropped his hands to his lap.

"What can I do?" he whispered. "I can't stay inside the house and lock the doors."

"No, you sure can't," Clint admitted. "None of us know what to do because we don't know what will happen or when it will happen, but I suggest that you carry a gun if you've got one."

"You want me to get killed fighting for Wallace's money?" Carney demanded.

"No, but it's possible you can hold them off until Ludlow and me get there. Or if it's just Fargo, you may need it to defend yourself."

Carney nodded and rose. "I'll get it," he said, and left the room.

Nan was staring at Clint as if she couldn't fully grasp the significance of what he had said. Now she leaned forward. "Who wrote that stuff on the barn?" she asked.

"We don't know," Clint said. "We wish we did. I didn't think Fargo had a friend in town, but he does. Whoever did the writing may help Fargo when the showdown comes. That scares me as much as anything. We've got a Judas with us. Since we don't know who he is, we don't know how to defend ourselves."

Nan was, Clint knew, a cool-headed, practical woman who wasn't frightened easily. It was one of the many things about her he admired. Now, after thinking about what he had just said, she rejected it.

"I don't believe there's any Judas in town," she said. "A kid or some fool with a sense of humor wrote it."

Clint shook his head. "I thought that when I first saw the writing, but I don't think so now. In the first place, even the kids take Fargo seriously enough not to do a fool trick like this. In the second place, this has been timed with the telegraph wires being down and no mail coming in since the stage got here Tuesday. I think some of Fargo's friends cut the wires and kept them cut so we couldn't send for help. We wouldn't even know about Fargo breaking out until he was ready to warn us. I think he's close enough to be in town by night. He'd have time if he'd made the break Monday."

"But why, Clint? Why would Fargo want to scare us? It just puts us on our guard. It would make more sense if he didn't warn us."

Clint leaned back in his chair and rolled a cigarette. He said slowly, "You've got to understand Fargo. He's the most vindictive man I ever knew. I went to school with him for several years. He was the kind you had to fight or he made life so miserable you wanted to shoot yourself. Once he almost had me licked and he'd have gouged my eyes out if the rest hadn't pulled him off. One time he skinned a dog alive just to see him suffer. I had a fight with him over that."

Nan's small hands clenched. "You're saying that he's the kind who makes people suffer just for fun?"

"That's it. I saw it in him time after time. He didn't change any after he grew up. Got worse if anything. He claims he was framed for stealing that calf. He might have been, but he'd done enough other things to spend the rest of his life in Canon City. Of course he wouldn't see it that way. It would be like him to kill everyone who had anything to do with sending him to the pen because he was innocent of the particular crime that sent him there."

She jumped up as her father came back into the room. "I'll be late," she said, and ran into her bedroom.

Carney sat down, his face gray. "I wish I had a drink," he said. "Trouble is, I couldn't stop if I started. I guess I've never been as scared in my life as I am right now. You know, Clint, this is another case of jumping when the Judge hollered. I never told you. Never told anyone, I guess. Well, the Judge said to me privately before the trial started that I'd better see to it that Fargo went up for stealing that calf. The way it turned out, there wasn't any question, the evidence being what it was.''

This was news to Clint. He considered it a moment, and then asked, ''Did the Judge tell you why he wanted Fargo convicted?''

''No, but we've heard the stories about Fargo's ranch being a hideout and him riding with Duke Wade's outfit or the Wild Bunch. You know how Wallace hates outlaws. I suppose he thought the world and San Lorenzo County in particular would be better off if Fargo was in prison.

That was probably true and Clint nodded. Then he said, ''Did it ever occur to you that Bill Ivor and Bonita lived down there close to Fargo's ranch and Wallace knew or guessed that Fargo was in love with Bonita?''

Carney nodded gravely. ''It certainly has.''

Clint dropped the subject, thinking that Carney wouldn't know for sure. ''Let's see your gun,'' he said.

Carney drew a pearl-handled .32 from his coat pocket. He said apologetically, ''It's small, but I'm not used to a big revolver. I don't shoot very well with this one, but I'd do worse with a .45.''

Clint handed it back. He had only contempt for a gun of that caliber, but this was Doug Carney's business. Besides, he was probably right about not being able to handle a bigger gun.

''Tom and me will be out of town until about noon,'' Clint said. ''If anything happens between now and then, you'll have to handle it alone.''

Alarmed, Carney cried, ''You can't do that. The town is defenseless.''

''There are men in San Lorenzo, and every one of them owns a gun. You can't always depend on a sheriff and his deputy, Doug.''

Carney stared at the table for a moment, then he raised his gaze to Clint's face. He had trouble controlling his voice as he said, ''When the Judge dies, Bonita will be rich. She'll keep me on at the bank because she doesn't have anyone else. I can promise you that the bank will give you a substantial loan if you want to buy your old ranch back. Or any other ranch on the mesa. You and Nan have had to put off your wedding too long."

Clint studied the banker's face, suspecting trickery. This was a complete reversal of Carney's previous attitude. The man was a habitual gambler—poker had a hold on him the way liquor had on some men. He owed money to Sam Calloway and Tom Ludlow and almost every other man who sat in on the big Saturday night games in the back room of the Gay Lady. The fact that he was the worst poker player in the county didn't keep him from coming back whenever he had a Saturday night that was free. The result was that he was always broke. Nan paid the taxes and the grocery bill and anything else that was needed to keep the home going.

"Thanks," Clint said. "I didn't know you felt that way, but we may have to wait a long time for Wallace to die."

"No we won't," Carney said quickly. "Fargo will kill him. If he doesn't, someone else will. You don't know how people hate him."

"I know," Clint said. "I'm one of them."

"Of course you are," Carney said, "but you aren't the kind who would kill the old bastard. Some of them are. Even if he doesn't get rubbed out, I want you to get back to ranching. If it comes to that, I'll personally loan you what you need."

This was the craziest thing Carney had said yet. Clint thought of saying that he knew Carney didn't have a nickel, but what was the use. Instead, he said, "I guess it would be to my profit to keep you alive."

"Indeed it would," Carney said.

Clint rose as Nan returned to the kitchen. "I'm ready," she said. "I'm late now."

Clint went out through the back door with her, saying

nothing more to Carney. The whole thing was too ridiculous to comment on. But when a man was as scared as Doug Carney, he was likely to say ridiculous things.

When they reached the school grounds, the bell was ringing. "Oh my," Nan said. "Mr. Delong will be mad again. It's eight-thirty, and I was supposed to be here fifteen minutes ago."

"Tell him I'm to blame." He kissed her, not caring whether the principal or school children or anyone else saw them. He said, "Tell Delong to keep an eye on Danny Tebo today."

She was startled by that. "You don't think . . ."

"That's exactly what I think. Danny Tebo's father was on the jury."

"I'll tell him," she said, and hurried into the schoolhouse.

It was not until Clint reached Main Street that he remembered he had forgotten to ask about Cousin Phil.

SIX

TOM LUDLOW WAITED AT THE LIVERY STABLE UNTIL FIVE minutes after eight, his horse saddled, his Winchester in the boot. His anxiety had grown steadily until it was unbearable. He had not taken more than two minutes to warn Sam Calloway, then he had hurried on to the livery stable. Clint shouldn't have been in the Carney house over five minutes, just long enough to tell the banker what had happened and come to the stable.

Ludlow paced up and down the runway, cursing Clint as the slow minutes dragged by. Shorty Bogardus stood in the doorway of his office watching Ludlow with an expression of virulent hatred. The sheriff noticed it and was surprised, for he knew of no reason for the stableman hating him. He then put it out of his mind.

One of Ludlow's assets was his ability to appraise men. He based his judgment partly on a man's wealth and power and status in the community, partly on the moral and physical strength of the man himself. Judge Wallace, of course, was high on Ludlow's appraisal sheet. Sam Calloway was nearly as high. Clint Harper, too, simply because the man had to be reckoned with in any situation which involved him.

Most of the town's men were leaners who could be thrust aside with a sharp word or threatening gesture. The pompous school principal, Kenneth Delong, was typical. Or Doug Carney, who would be a big fat zero if he wasn't hooked up with Judge Wallace. Shorty Bogardus, too, fitted in this category. Let him get his back humped. He'd be a nuisance, no more, a gnat buzzing in a man's ear.

So Ludlow fidgeted the seconds away, walking around, checking his gun, looking at his watch every minute. Finally he could wait no longer. Clint Harper could go when he pleased. He was probably sitting in the Carney house holding hands with Nan, as moonstruck as a school kid having his first love affair.

"Tell Harper I've left," Ludlow said. "He'll know where I've gone. And tell him to hustle. I want him back in town by noon."

Shorty didn't move, his bitter expression did not change. Ludlow mounted and rode into the street, further irritated by Shorty's sullen manner. He waved to Sam Calloway who was sweeping off the walk in front of the store, nodded at Pete Larson who stepped through the batwings to throw a bucket of dirty water into the street in front of the Gay Lady, and a moment later spoke to Doc Julian who was leaving his house, his black bag in his hand. Maybe Mrs. Delong's baby was finally getting here.

The town was behind him then and he let his horse go. The animal had not been ridden for several days and wanted to run. Presently Ludlow pulled him down and kept him at a steady pace, taking the road that led directly east toward the Cloud Mountains that rose ahead of him, sharp granite peaks raking the sky. They still held most of their winter snows. It was a beautiful sight which he often enjoyed, but he had too many worries this morning to admire scenery.

The town had been peaceful enough this morning. So was the land, running almost level for miles on both sides of the road. Good grass and not much sagebrush, with here and there a small cedar and an occasional group of ranch buildings.

The road followed Cougar Creek, a willow-lined stream that was still low at this time of year, awaiting the spring run-off. Gradually the country began to lift, more sage-brush now, and more cedars. Cattle were grazing on both sides of the road. A few horses. He saw a bunch of riders leave one of the ranches. A band of school kids riding toward the Cougar Creek school passed him; he spoke to them and they returned his greeting, and rode on, some of them staring curiously at him.

It was all so damned peaceful and ordinary that it sent a prickle down his spine. If he only had enough foresight to know what was going to happen and when it would happen! He didn't have the slightest doubt that there would be hell to pay within another twenty-four hours, probably within the next twelve. He finally, then, came to grips with the problem that had been in the back of his mind since early morning when Clint had told him about the writing on the stable door. What would he do when the trouble broke?

Ludlow was seldom honest with anyone else, but he was always honest with himself. He could lie beautifully to Marge Rainer, telling her how much he loved her and promising to marry her. She believed him; she was starved for love and had turned to him because he had built his relationship with her slowly and carefully.

At times he had been tempted by the prospect of marrying her. She had some money, she was a good cook, a fine housekeeper, and an excellent bed partner. But he had never stayed in any place more than a few years. When his term was over he'd drift on again.

No, a wife was out of the question, so the temptation to marry Marge had never become a very strong one. Even now he was on occasion a little bored by Marge, but the habit of going over to see her was hard to break and he'd probably keep on seeing her as long as he was in San Lorenzo.

He reached a long hill, where the creek dropped into a steep-walled canyon. At this point the main road turned north toward the San Lorenzo River, keeping west of the foothills of the Cloud Mountains, but he continued east, following a side road that would take him to Matt Smith's ranch.

Once more Ludlow brought his wandering thoughts back to the problem that worried him. What would he do when Fargo showed up? He had followed the basic principle that it was better to be a live coward than a dead hero, a principle that would not appeal to the people who elected him. The trick, of course, was to maneuver in such a manner that no one would think him a coward, a trick which he thought he had mastered well.

When he started serving his first term, he had been fortunate in hiring a deputy named Al Seigal, a tough hand who had been a little too eager to use his gun on occasion and who stayed on the job because he enjoyed the status that wearing a star gave him. Ludlow, with Judge Wallace's help, had been forced more than once to whitewash Seigal after a killing. Seigal had been his deputy when Fargo was arrested.

Now that he looked back on it, Ludlow was surprised at the ease with which Ben Fargo had been taken. Perhaps it had been because the man actually was innocent and thought he would be acquitted. But Wallace had been determined the man be convicted and sent to prison, and he was.

After the trial Fargo was a wild man. Ludlow didn't know what he'd have done if he hadn't had Seigal for a deputy. On at least two occasions Seigal had gone into Fargo's cell and pistol-whipped him, but even that had not taken the fight out of the outlaw. You'd have to kill him to do that, and now Ludlow wished they had.

A few months after the trial Seigal had got himself shot to death in a gun fight in the Gay Lady. For a time Ludlow had no deputy because he couldn't find the right man, and all the time he was worrying that he'd have to face some kind of serious trouble without a deputy.

Then the bank had taken Clint Harper's ranch. Ludlow knew Clint, having watched him in several fights and had him on two posses. He offered the deputy's star to Clint, and with jobs as scarce as they were, Clint accepted.

Ludlow had been foolish to say anything to Clint about firing him. He wouldn't have said it if Clint hadn't come into Marge's bedroom and caught him there. Knowing how Clint felt about Marge, Ludlow was sure it wouldn't set well. Actually he wouldn't have been surprised if Clint had hauled him out of bed and licked hell out of him. Fear as much as anger had made him blurt out that Clint was fired, and now he was thankful he'd been given a chance to back up.

In many ways Clint Harper puzzled him. He was a better deputy than Al Seigal had ever been because he didn't use his gun unless he had to. He was smart, and he had more cold courage in a pinch than any other man Ludlow had ever seen. But he was stupidly honest, and he was equally stupid about things that didn't really matter, like a woman's reputation. Ludlow didn't doubt that Clint would do what he had threatened if Ludlow got Marge into trouble and didn't marry her.

He topped the slope, the creek making a rumble to his right as it fell a sheer hundred feet over a rock ledge. Matt Smith's ranch lay in front of him, its hay meadows spread a mile or more on each side of the creek. Smith's barns and outbuildings were tight and well built, but the house was little more than a shack.

Here was something which Ludlow did not understand. Matt Smith was a queer one, so perhaps there was no explanation. More than once Ludlow had heard that the rancher had a fortune hidden here somewhere. Doug Carney said that Smith never deposited a dollar in the bank, and the men who worked for Smith bragged about how he always paid them in gold. Why should a man live out here by himself when he could afford a housekeeper? Even if he liked being alone, why would he live in a shack that was hardly fit for a poverty-stricken squatter in the broken, red rock country south of San Lorenzo?

Ludlow rode to the house and dismounted. He still hadn't decided what he'd do tonight, or this afternoon if Fargo showed up then. Clint could be depended upon to take care of his end of it, but if it stacked up the way Ludlow expected, it was a job for more than one man.

Well, maybe he could think of a legitimate reason to leave town. Perhaps ride to Fargo's old ranch to see if anyone was there. The trouble was he'd jump out of the frying pan into the fire if he ran into some of Fargo's friends.

As he walked across the hard-packed dirt of the front yard to the door, he saw that it was open. That seemed surprising, for it was a cold day, colder here next to the mountains than it had been when he'd left San Lorenzo nearly two hours before. Smith might be in the barn or one of the outbuildings. Ludlow decided he'd knock and then look around. Smith might be gone. If he was, Ludlow would leave a note and ride back to San Lorenzo.

He stopped in the doorway, gasping hoarsely. He gripped the door casing, and his knees threatened to buckle under him. Fargo had beaten him here. Smith lay on his belly in the middle of the room.

Slowly Ludlow walked to him, and kneeling, saw that he had been shot in the back. It must have been done some time ago, or he would have heard the shot. But maybe not. He couldn't have heard it if it happened when he was close to the falls. He lifted Smith's arm and felt for the pulse. Nothing. The man was dead, but the body was still warm.

Suddenly the thought hit Ludlow that Fargo might be here now. It paralyzed him even before he heard a floor board squeak behind him. He knew he should pull his gun and whirl; he might get in a lucky shot. But fear froze him there in the middle of the room. He sat huddled beside Smith's body, unable to move.

Then the roof fell on him and he toppled forward on his face. He did not hear the wall clock strike ten o'clock.

Seven

At twenty-five minutes before nine Sam Calloway saw Clint striding along the board walk toward the livery stable. He stepped through the street door of the store and motioned Clint to come in. Clint hesitated, knowing that Ludlow would be impatient and angry because of the delay. Apparently Calloway read his mind, for he shouted, "Tom's gone. Come on over here. I've got something to tell you."

Clint crossed the street, thinking it was like Ludlow to go on. He'd want to get to Smith's ranch and be back in town before Fargo showed up. He wouldn't want the outlaw to catch him alone out in the cedars. Not that it made any difference when Ludlow left. They were going in opposite directions, so there was no reason for them to leave at the same time. But the point was that he'd want Clint here when he got back.

When Clint stepped up on the walk in front of the store, he asked, "How long ago did Tom leave?"

"Oh, maybe half an hour," Calloway said, and stepped back out of the doorway. "Come on in. What I've got to say won't take long. Tom stopped here to tell me about the writing and said he was going to warn Matt Smith and you were riding out to the toll bridge to see Bill Ivor, then he went high-tailing on to the stable."

If Ludlow had left half an hour ago, Clint thought as he followed Calloway to the rear of the store, he'd be back in town by noon. If Clint wasn't here then, Ludlow would storm around like a bear with a sore tail. Clint grinned as he considered it. If Ludlow started cussing him, he'd throw his star on the ground and walk off. Then Ludlow could see where he stood. He'd do anything to keep from facing Fargo alone when the outlaw rode into town, but if he didn't watch his temper, that's exactly what he'd be doing.

Calloway had a huge, rolltop desk and a couple of chairs in one corner in the back of the room. He motioned for Clint to take one of the chairs, then he picked up a box of cigars from the top of his desk, offered them to Clint who took one, then placed the box back where it had been.

Calloway sat down, his face deeply lined by worry, then he muttered, "Hell, I didn't get one myself. That shows the condition I'm in."

He got up, took a cigar from the box, bit off the end, and lighted it. Sitting down again, he said, "Clint, this is a bad thing, a damned bad thing."

Clint pulled on his cigar and waited. Sam Calloway was one man in San Lorenzo, maybe the only man, who could be counted on not to do something crazy. He was tall and slightly stooped, with a splash of white showing at his temples. He had a wife and eight children, he made a good living out of his store, and was one of the few men in the county who could get along with Judge Wallace and still retain the friendship of the ranchers who hated Wallace.

Calloway took the cigar out of his mouth, inspected the ash, and then said somberly, "This is like a bad dream you have over and over until you know it's really going to happen. Two years ago I sat in the jury box with Doug Carney and Shorty Bogardus and the rest, and heard Ben Fargo swear he'd get out of the pen and come back and kill all of us. There wasn't the slightest doubt in my mind but what he'd do it. Or try. The only difference between the way it is and the way I thought it would be is that I didn't think we'd be warned."

"You know why we were warned?"

Calloway nodded. "Fargo's squeezing all the fun out of us he can. The part that fooled me was that I didn't think anyone was a good enough friend of his to take a chance on doing that writing." He pulled on the cigar, his chair canted back against the wall. "A lot of things could happen. It's dry and if a wind comes up tonight, he might burn the town. I'm thinking about my wife and kids. I'm afraid to leave 'em in town, but I'm more afraid to take 'em anywhere else."

Clint shook his head. "I think he aims to ride in, rob the bank, do the killing he thinks he's got to do, and strike out for the Utah line."

Calloway smiled wryly. "Fargo's a mad dog, Clint. You know it and I know it. If he was just a plain ornery outlaw, you could make a reasonable guess what he'd do, but with him you can't. The question is what you're going to do."

"What do you mean by that?"

"Tom Ludlow thinks he fools us, and I guess he does fool most people, but not me. When the shooting starts, he'll be hiding under the bed. That leaves it up to you. You've got no reason to love the Judge. Or Doug Carney even if he is Nan's father, so I couldn't blame you if you went fishing."

Clint chewed on his cigar, remembering that only a minute or so ago he had been telling himself that if Ludlow started cussing him, he'd hand in his star. He said, "Sam, sometimes I think you're a mind reader and it scares me." He hesitated, then he added, "I guess I'll be around no matter what happens."

"I figured you would," Calloway said. "I'm no mind reader. It's just that I know how I'd feel if I was in your boots, working under a man like Tom Ludlow. Anyhow, I feel better hearing you say that. If you need me, you know where to find me."

"We'll need you, all right," Clint said. "I'm assuming that Fargo won't show up this morning. That's why I'm leaving town. I could send someone to tell Bill Ivor, but I want to talk to him. Maybe you'd better keep a gun handy."

Calloway nodded. "I'll sure do that. Now I guess I'd better tell you what I called you in for. As postmaster, I suppose I shouldn't mention this, but I'm going to anyhow. It might be important. If you don't think it is, forget it."

He hesitated, scratching the back of his neck, then apparently decided he couldn't back up now, so he hurried on, "In the two years since Fargo's been in the pen, about a dozen letters have come to Marge Rainer. Judging from the handwriting and the postmark, I'm sure they're from Ben Fargo."

Clint took the cigar out of his mouth and stared at Calloway. If anyone else had told him that, he'd have called the man a liar. But not Sam Calloway. He said hoarsely, "You're wrong, Sam. You've got to be. I know Marge. She wouldn't have anything to do with Ben Fargo."

"That's what I thought. I know Marge, too. I like her. She's a fine, straightforward woman. But I'm not wrong. I had some correspondence with Fargo once. He owed me a bill I was trying to collect. I got one of his letters out and compared the handwriting to what was on the envelopes coming to Marge. The same man wrote them, Clint."

Clint had been impatient to finish talking and get started for the toll bridge, but now he forgot all about Bill Ivor.

He said, "I'll ask Marge. She won't lie to me."

"I thought that's what you'd want to do. Like I said, it may not be important, but I've been sitting on it so long I had to tell you."

Clint rose, more upset by this information than anything that had happened since Shorty Bogardus had shaken him awake that morning. He said, "Keep your eyes peeled," and left the store.

He went directly to Marge's house, churning this around in his mind and not coming up with any answers. It was one of those things which was simply impossible. He didn't think Marge even knew Fargo.

He found her kneading bread dough on the kitchen table. She motioned for him to sit down and kept on working, not able to meet his gaze. She had been crying again. It wasn't that she was sorry because of what she'd done, he thought, but simply that she'd been found out.

"I guess you're a good man, Clint," she said in a low voice. "I suppose that you and Nan have never done anything wrong no matter how much you were in love, but I'm not made that way, and Tom isn't, either. If what we've been doing is a sin . . ."

"Marge," he broke in, "I'm not judging you, and I'm not going around telling everyone. I said what I did this morning because I know Tom Ludlow. He's not fit to be in the same room with you. He'll break your heart, I tell you."

"I guess that's the chance any woman takes with a man," she said.

"I didn't come here to talk about that," he said. "I've given you some advice. You can take it or leave it. I'm here this time about something else. Sam Calloway tells me you've been getting letters from Ben Fargo. I want to know why."

She looked up from the dough, shocked, then she stepped back from the table and sat down. "I haven't,

Clint. For heaven's sake, what would I have to do with an outlaw like him? Why, it's the most . . ." She stopped, her face going blank. She whispered, "Oh."

"Go ahead. Tell me about it."

"I can't, Clint. I know now what Calloway's talking about, but the letters weren't for me."

"I've got to know, Marge. I don't care what promises you've made, you've got to tell me. It may mean the lives of a dozen people in this town."

She stared at her flour-covered hands that lay clasped on her lap. "All right, I guess I do have to tell you. The letters were for Bonita. I've never read any of them, so I don't know what they're about. I don't even know for sure who they're from. I mean, she never told me. I haven't had one for almost two months, so they can't have anything to do with Fargo breaking out of the pen."

"How'd they happen to come to you?"

"Bonita asked me to let them come to me because she was afraid the Judge would get one of them out of the post office. You know what he'd do. There was always a small envelope inside the big one. I'd open the big one. The one inside would have Bonita written on it. Nothing else."

"She never told you anything about what was in them?"

"Not a thing. I never asked her because I didn't think it was any of my business. I've felt awfully sorry for her, married to that old man. The kind of man he is, too. Well, when she asked me to do it, I didn't see any harm in it, and if it would make her life a little easier, or happier . . ."

Clint rose. "I'm not blaming you, Marge, but I've got to talk to Bonita. I'm riding out to the toll bridge now. You see Bonita and have her here in your house around one. I'll be back before that."

"I don't know, Clint," Marge said hesitantly. "Bonita made me promise not to tell anybody. Now if I go up there and tell her I . . ."

"She's going to be a lot madder if I go up there," he said. "That's what I'll do if she won't come here. This is something we can't fool with. We don't even know how much time we've got. Maybe she won't be able to tell me anything, but I've got to find out."

"All right," Marge said. "I'll talk to her."

Once at the stable, it took Clint a moment to saddle his gelding, a leggy bay that had been his favorite mount when he'd been on the ranch. Shorty Bogardus, standing in the runway, said, "Ludlow was in a hell of a hurry this morning. Walked around like he had ants in his pants waiting for you. Said for you to get a hustle on."

Clint backed his horse into the runway. "If he gets back before I do, tell him I'll try to get to town by noon." He glanced at his watch. A quarter after nine. His bay was faster than Ludlow's horse. He should make it with time to spare. Actually it didn't matter whether he got back before Ludlow did or not. The question was whether he should leave town at all, but he might save Bill Ivor's life if he got there in time.

"You got a gun here?" Clint asked.

"A shotgun," Shorty answered. "I guess it wouldn't be no help."

"It might," Clint said. "One more thing. The story's probably all over town by now, or soon will be. People are going to get jumpy. If anything happens before I get back, Sam Calloway's the man to run things."

Shorty watched him mount and leave town in a gallop. He walked along the runway to the back of the stable and stared at Marge Rainer's house. Damn Tom Ludlow!

Eight

Duke Wade stood looking down at Ludlow's motionless body for a long moment, his gun still in his hand. Then he dropped the Colt back into his holster and turned Ludlow over on his back. He was afraid he'd hit the lawman too hard with the barrel of his gun, but when he picked up the sheriff's wrist, he felt a pulse, strong and steady. A hard skull, he thought, which was exactly what Ben Fargo had always said about Ludlow, a thick head and no guts.

Wade had never been in San Lorenzo County before except for the few times when he'd holed up with his bunch on Fargo's ranch. He had never seen Ludlow before, but from Fargo's description, he was sure that this man was the sheriff.

For a time he considered killing Ludlow, then decided against it. Fargo would be sore if he did. Fargo had said repeatedly that Ludlow was his meat. The sheriff would pay and pay plenty for the cuffing around Fargo had been given when he was in the San Lorenzo jail. The only thing Fargo seemed to regret was that he couldn't make Seigal pay. The man had been stupid enough to get himself killed.

Wade gripped Ludlow by the shoulder and dragged him through the kitchen into a storeroom in the rear of the house. He stepped back into the kitchen, closed the door, and gave the turn pin a twist. The main thing now was to keep Ludlow from getting a look at him. He had some things to attend to in San Lorenzo before Fargo rode into town.

Ludlow had interrupted his search for Smith's money. He had just finished looking in the bedroom when he'd heard the sheriff ride up. Now he started in on the kitchen. It didn't seem a likely place, although a man as whacky as this Smith might hide his dinero anywhere, even in the bottom of a half-filled sack of flour.

Wade was thorough and destructive, emptying every sack and can on the floor. He checked the pantry, he looked under the table for a secret shelf or drawer, he even examined the oven of the big range. He found nothing, and he began to wonder if Fargo might have been mistaken about Smith's hidden fortune.

Next he attacked the front room, ripping the leather cover off the couch, upsetting the furniture and looking underneath, and finally examining the walls of the three rooms. Nothing.

He scratched his head, wondering if it was worth while to tear up the floor. Smith might have buried the money in his yard, or hidden it in the barn or one of the sheds, but that seemed unlikely. If a man was crazy enough to hide his money, he'd probably be crazy enough to hide it where he could count it and look at it. Besides, Smith would have been afraid it would be stolen while he was asleep. No, it was probably right here in the house.

Ludlow had come to and was trying to force the door of the storeroom. Wade swore, and walking to the storeroom, said in a falsetto voice, "Cut it out." The racket stopped. Wade listened for a moment until he was sure Ludlow was going to quiet down, then he went out through the back door to the tool shed, found a crowbar, and returned to the house.

He examined the floor carefully, tapping with the crowbar. If Smith had torn the boards up and nailed them down again each time he added money to his hoard, they would have been splintered and would show an extraordinary number of hammer marks, but he didn't find anything of the sort. He stood in the middle of the front room, looking around and trying to think of something he had overlooked. He shouldn't have killed Smith until he got the location of the money out of him, but he hadn't thought it would be hard to find. Now if he showed up without the money at the line cabin where Fargo was hiding, he'd get a good cussing.

The only place he hadn't looked was the fireplace. If he didn't find it there, he might just as well be on his way. It would take days to examine the yard and outbuildings thoroughly, and he didn't have that much time. With Fargo, he had planned the entire operation carefully, allowing only a few hours for this side venture.

He hammered each stone of the fireplace without any luck, and then, in desperation, he pried up the hearthstone. It was a heavy piece of flagstone, so heavy that he almost gave up before he had it upended. Smith had been a big man, but even so, it was too much work to lift the hearthstone just to play with his money.

After several minutes of heaving and sweating, Wade finally had the stone on its edge. He stepped back and, wiping his forehead with his sleeve, permitted himself a grin. There it was, as neat as you please, half a dozen canvas bags, each one pleasingly plump and securely tied with buckskin thongs.

He glanced at the clock on the wall. Five minutes before

twelve. Fargo had told him to leave by noon whether he had the money or not. Going into the pantry, he found a couple of flour sacks. He hastily dropped some biscuits and a piece of roast beef into one, and, taking the other into the front room, lifted the sacks of gold from their hiding place and dropped them into it.

Going to the storeroom door, he said in the falsetto tone he'd used before, "Wait for an hour, then you can bust the door open and ride back to town. Tell 'em. Fargo will be along after a while."

He returned to the front room, picked up the two flour sacks, and left the house, laughing aloud as he pictured Ludlow, abjectly sitting on the floor in the storeroom while he waited for the hour to pass. A poor excuse for a sheriff, that Tom Ludlow.

Wade walked to the shed where he had hidden his horse, tied the sacks behind the saddle, mounted, rode down the creek. According to Fargo, the only man who would give them any trouble was Ludlow's deputy, Clint Harper. All the way from Canon City, Fargo had talked about the men he was going to kill for putting him through two years of hell.

Fargo was like an Indian the way he hated a man. He said he was going to start with Judge Wallace. He'd said very little about Clint Harper, but Wade had the notion that Fargo hated the deputy almost as much as he hated Wallace.

Wade scratched a bearded cheek as he thought about it. To him revenge had never been important. He'd made a bad guess when he'd led his bunch into Trinidad and held up a bank. He'd been shot all to hell and several of his men killed. The rest had scattered. He didn't know where they were now except for Muley Hanks who was supposed to keep the wire cut between San Lorenzo and Grand Junction. After the holdup, Wade had been sent to Canon

City and was there to welcome Fargo when he showed up.

They had talked their future over many times, planning a break which had never come off while Wade was there. They had also planned what Wade would do to help Fargo get out of the country if Wade was free when Fargo broke out. They had even gone over the Trinidad failure, Fargo pointing out the mistakes Wade had made. Mostly it had been a matter of improper timing. He'd been too cocky, Fargo said. It never paid to take anything for granted. In view of the way it had turned out, Wade couldn't very well argue the matter.

When the opportunity to break out had come, several months after Wade's release, Fargo had escaped with half a dozen other men. They'd scattered, and Fargo headed for the river where Wade was waiting with two good horses, guns, and a change of clothes. The rest had probably been captured by now, but not Fargo. Worn out by the hard ride, he was asleep in the line cabin back in the cedars. He hadn't been in good shape. He was lucky to have been able to stay in the saddle as long as he had. He'd been beaten up too many times by one of the guards, but for some strange reason, Fargo didn't hate him. The San Lorenzo men who had sent him up were the ones Fargo hated.

And Fargo's hatred for some of the San Lorenzo men was understandable. Judge Wallace, for instance. He'd talk for an hour straight hand running about the old man and what he'd do to him. He dismissed Doug Carney as being a soft banker, and Ludlow as a bluff who depended on a tough deputy. But the part that bothered Wade was Fargo's failure to discuss Harper. He kept his reasons for hating the deputy locked up within himself.

When Wade reached the main road, he swung north for half a mile, then turned east into the cedars toward the line cabin. He thought of going on and leaving Fargo and his consuming hunger for revenge. Now that he had Smith's money, he could pay Hanks off and still have a chunk of dinero left. But he couldn't do it. Foolish by Fargo's standards, but not by his. To Duke Wade, loyalty was a tie that was not easily broken, and that, Wade realized, was one of the differences between him and Ben Fargo.

Wade found Fargo asleep in the line cabin. Wade shook him awake, showed him the gold, and dumped the biscuits and roast beef on the blanket beside Fargo. He said, "I'd better get moving. It took longer than I figured."

Fargo got to his feet, grimacing from the soreness that the hard ride had given him. His pale face had taken on a lean, wolfish expression. He'd always had some of that appearance, but it was exaggerated now, tired and half starved as he was, and with a heavy growth of stubble on his face. His light brown eyes had a way of darting around like those of a hunted animal, not fixing on anything for more than a moment.

Now, aware of this quality in Fargo more than ever, Wade felt his doubts grow. He asked bluntly, "What about this man Harper?"

Fargo had sat down on his blanket and was eating ravenously. They hadn't been able to find enough food to satisfy him since they'd left Canon City. He hadn't been filled up since he'd gone to prison, he said. He just couldn't eat the slop they gave him. Wade had never found it that bad, but judging from the way Fargo had thinned down, he hadn't been eating.

Fargo, his mouth full, motioned to the biscuits and roast beef. "Go ahead and eat, man. It ain't no banquet, but it'll do."

Wade shook his head. "I'll make out till I get to town. I want to know about Harper."

Fargo sliced off another hunk of beef and popped it into his mouth. For all the world he looked like a starving coyote who had stumbled upon a steer carcass. He said, "You claimed you was in a hurry. Get moving. I'll wait till the sun's about down. I oughta get to town between nine and ten o'clock. I'll see you at Doug Carney's house."

"Ben," Wade said doggedly, "you're going to tell me about Harper or I ain't budging out of this cabin."

Fargo chewed and swallowed, then picked up his canteen and took a drink. "All right," he said, "I'll tell you. I'm going to hurt him and hurt him bad. I'll start with the Carney girl." He shook the knife blade in Wade's direction. "I'll fix her face so Harper won't recognize her. Then we'll turn her loose and she'll go to him and he'll come after me. That's when I'll get him."

Wade, squatting here in the gloom of the cabin, stared at Fargo's pale, weasel-thin face, and felt a strange prickling along his spine. He had ridden the owlhoot trail since he was fifteen. He was twenty-nine now. Fourteen years of it. The only time he hadn't been riding with a bunch of ridge runners was when he'd been in the pen. Plenty of his fellow prisoners had been sneaking, knife-using bastards he wouldn't trust to get behind him, but he had never, in all the years he had ridden with outlaws or been in prison, seen an expression of complete, animal viciousness like what he saw now on Ben Fargo's face.

"No," Wade said. "Not the Carney girl."

"Who says I can't?"

"I do," Wade said. "Ben, you're hating so much you ain't thinking straight. Our job is to clean out San Lorenzo and be on our way. It don't make no big difference whether you get square with men like Wallace and Ludlow or not. It's the money that's important."

"To you," Fargo said. "Not to me." He made a sweeping gesture with his knife blade as if to dismiss the whole argument. "And another thing. Find out where the Tebo kid is. His pa was on that jury."

Wade shook his head. He said sourly, "I helped you because we used to ride together, Ben. And I'll admit I thought it would be easy pickings in San Lorenzo. I figured it wouldn't hurt if you rubbed old Wallace out. Ludlow, too. But when it comes to a woman and a boy, you can ride your way and I'll ride mine."

Fargo stopped chewing and stared at Wade, his pale eyes narrowed, the right corner of his mouth twitching with the regularity of a pulse beat. For a moment Wade thought Fargo was going for his gun, then he said, "All right, Duke. Maybe the money is what's important, but you ain't talking me out of killing Clint Harper."

"Why?" Wade shouted. "Damn it, he wasn't even on the jury."

"Because he used to beat hell out of me when we were kids," Fargo shouted back. "And because he used to take my girls away from me when we got older. I thought Bonita was one girl who would stick with me whether she was married to old man Wallace or not, but now she says she don't want nothing more to do with me. I figure Harper's to blame for that, too."

"Maybe it's something else," Wade said. "Maybe you hate every lawman, hate 'em enough to kill 'em."

"That's right, too," Fargo said defiantly. "In San Lorenzo anyway. If I didn't want to kill Harper before, I sure do now that he's wearing one of Ludlow's tin stars." He motioned toward the door. "Like you said, you ain't got much time."

Wade moved to the door, then looked back. Fargo had picked up the piece of roast beef and was gnawing on it like a dog.

Leaving the cabin, Wade mounted and rode downslope through the cedars toward the county road. He had seen prison change men, but never as much as it had changed Fargo, and the odd part of it was that most of the change had come during the last few months, after Wade had been released.

Again he was tempted to ride on, but now it was not even an attractive thought. He had left Smith's money with Fargo. He couldn't afford to ride out with empty pockets, now that he had put this much time and money into Fargo's escape.

Fargo had assured him there was fifty thousand dollars or more in San Lorenzo just waiting to be picked up. He'd play it out, Wade told himself, and hope Ben Fargo would remember that money, not revenge, was their principal objective. He had come a long ways down, Wade thought bitterly. Once, like Butch Cassidy, he had been one of the top men in the outlaw world, but now he was just an ex-con, his fate tied up with a mad-dog killer who wanted to take his hate out on a boy named Danny Tebo and a girl named Nan Carney who was in love with Clint Harper. A hell of a note and no mistake.

He glanced up at the sun. After one, he judged, which meant that it would be three or later before he reached San Lorenzo.

Nine

Clint left San Lorenzo at a brisk pace, taking the road to the toll bridge. It angled a little west of north as far as Judge Wallace's Box W. At that point it swung sharply to the northwest, bisecting the peninsula known as Land's End that was formed by the Dolores and San Lorenzo rivers. The toll bridge crossed the San Lorenzo just above the junction of the two rivers.

On impulse, Clint stopped at the Box W and found Wallace's foreman, Irish Mike O'Brien, in the little stone building beside the ranch house which served as an office. O'Brien had worked for Wallace in one capacity or another for more than ten years. He was a squat, broad-shouldered man who constantly nursed a clay pipe, got drunk every Saturday night in the Gay Lady, and was always on the job Monday morning. He had red hair and so many freckles they seemed to overlap, and a face that was as Irish as his name.

O'Brien was completely loyal to Wallace, having

learned a long time ago that the only way to get along with the old man was blindly to obey orders. As Clint stood in front of O'Brien's desk he knew he was wasting time stopping here. But now that he had stopped, he doggedly told O'Brien what had happened, all the time sensing that the foreman was impatient for him to be on his way.

"Ludlow and me can't guard everybody," Clint finished. "We need your help."

"Do you now?" O'Brien said. "Well, Harper, you're paid to enforce the law. I'm paid to run this spread. I ain't asking for help to do my job, so don't ask for none to do yours."

This was a typical reaction of a Wallace man, each of whom in his own way took on some of the arrogance which was so much a part of the Judge. Angered, Clint flared, "Damn it, Irish, you know there isn't another cowman in the county who cares what happens to the town or the Judge. If I can't get help from you, I can't get it from nobody. The rest of 'em hate him so much they'd just as soon see him dead."

O'Brien nodded. "That may be. They're a bunch of yellow bellies. They suck around after the Judge to his face and vote the way he tells 'em, and all the time they're hating him and everything he does."

"Doesn't it make any difference to you what happens to the Judge?"

"You bet it does. Not because I love the old booger. I don't guess he wants to be loved. He just wants to be obeyed." O'Brien took the pipe out of his mouth and pointed the stem at Clint. "That's the whole thing in a nutshell. I like this job and I want to keep it. Unless I get an order from the Judge to come to town and look out for him, I stay here. I'd lose my job if I done anything different."

It was true, Clint knew. He couldn't honestly blame

O'Brien. He turned and walked to the door, then stopped and looked back. "Have you or your crew seen any strangers ride by here since Monday noon?"

"I ain't," O'Brien said. "If the boys have, they didn't mention it to me."

Clint went out, mounted, and rode on toward the toll bridge, thinking what a hell of a nightmare this was. The feeling had grown on him since he had looked at those three words on Shorty Bogardus' livery stable door shortly after dawn. Not that he cared what happened to Judge Wallace, but other people, innocent people, would get hurt before this was over. Bonita maybe. And young Danny Tebo. Possibly even Nan. With Tom Ludlow the man he was, Clint Harper was the only protection these people had. Sam Calloway would give some help. Except for him, there was none.

The land ran on for miles, nearly level here except for a few brush-choked arroyos, and well covered by grass. No greasewood on this part of the range, very little sage-brush, and only a few cedars. He reached the edge of the canyon of the San Lorenzo, the road following a series of switchbacks to the river. Even so, the grade was so steep coming up from the bridge that the freighters had to bring half a load up at a time, a situation which gave the Judge a chance to double the rates on everything coming in from Grand Junction.

From the edge of the plateau, Clint could see a maze of canyons and red slickrock rims until they melted together in the distance, but once he dropped over the edge, the north wall of the San Lorenzo canyon cut off the view. Down in the bottom of the trench, the sky became a blue slit overhead.

Clint loved the feel of the wind in his face, the sight of the jagged peaks to the east and west, and the great distances which were so much a part of this country. He could not understand how Bill Ivor stood it in the bottom of the canyon, with the ragged sandstone walls closing him in. To Clint it would have been as bad as going to prison, but apparently it did not affect Ivor that way.

Clint reined up in front of the small house which stood near the southern approach to the bridge. Bill Ivor had been working in his garden above the bridge. Seeing Clint, he dropped his hoe and walked toward him.

Spring always came early down here. Looking at the grass and the leaves of the cottonwoods, it seemed to Clint that the season was a full month ahead of what it was on the mesa.

"What fetches you all the way out here, Clint?" Ivor asked as he held out his hand.

Clint had dismounted. Now he took Ivor's hand, thinking he had never seen a man change the way Ivor had after getting the job here at the toll bridge. He said, "Trouble, Bill."

When Ivor had lived with Bonita in the barren, redrock country south of town, he had been about as useless as a man could be. Lazy, dirty, unshaven, he had been without either pride or ambition. His daughter was his only asset.

Clint guessed that Wallace had laid down a few rules when he'd given Ivor the job. At any rate, Ivor was a changed man. He was clean, he dressed well, and he shaved every day. Even more important was his willingness to work. His garden was the best in the county, he kept the inside of the house as clean as a woman would have done, and he stayed on the job.

Ivor looked at Clint quizzically, his thumbs hooked under his belt. He was about fifty, a thin, medium-tall man who somewhere had found both pride and ambition. He said, "Bad trouble?"

"Plenty bad," Clint said. He told him about it, adding, "You'd better come to town for a few days. If Fargo should ride in this way, he'll stop long enough to kill you."

Ivor was scared. He wheeled and walked away from Clint to the bank of the river and stood staring down at the swift stream, gray with tailings from the mines in the mountains near its head. Presently he swung around.

"I can't leave here, Clint," he said. "I wish I could, but I've got to stay and hope Fargo will come in from the east. I figure he will, that being closer'n this side to Canon City."

"It's a fair guess," Clint agreed. "Well, you're the one who has to decide. I just thought you ought to be warned."

"Thank you kindly," Ivor said. "I appreciate you taking this ride for nothing, but you see . . ." He stopped, searching for words that didn't come easily, then he went on, "You see, I spent most of my life amounting to a little less'n nothing, then Bonita married the Judge and I guess the old man couldn't stand me for a father-in-law. Not the way I was, so he gave me this job. Now if I went off and left it, he wouldn't lose no money to speak of, but I'd sure as hell lose my job."

Clint nodded, thinking that Ivor was right just as Irish O'Brien had been right. He said, "Well, now you know, so keep your eyes open."

Ivor jerked his head at the house. "Come on in. I've got a bottle of whisky I save for important visitors."

"Thanks, but I've got to get back." Clint studied Ivor, not wanting to ask the question that had been nagging him, but he decided to ask it anyway. "Bill, were Bonita and Fargo in love before she married the Judge?"

Ivor got red in the face. He opened his mouth and closed it. He chewed on his lower lip, and then demanded, "Why do you ask?"

"Seems that Fargo and Bonita have been writing to each other after he went to the pen. I've been wondering if it had anything to do with him coming back."

Ivor kicked at a chunk of red sandstone that had fallen

from the south rim. "The fool," he said hoarsely. "The damned bitchy little fool."

"Well?"

Ivor looked at Clint defiantly. "Yeah, they were in love. I knew what he was. I told her, but she never believed nothing I said. We lived just north of him a piece. I've seen some of the worst outlaws in the country ride past my place to hide out with him. Or to get grub and trade for a fresh horse. Duke Wade. Butch Cassidy. Kid Curry. A lot of 'em."

Ivor swallowed and shook his head. "It wasn't just that he gave them owlhooters a hideout. More'n once he took off with Wade and his bunch and was gone for a week. I reckon they held up a bank or a train, but not in Colorado. He didn't want the law after him in this state. When the calf-stealing business came up, he surrendered without making a fight because he wanted to be cleared."

"Maybe he was innocent."

"I figure he was," Ivor agreed, "but he sure belonged in the pen. He's a bad one, Clint, the worst I ever seen. A damned Apache. That's what he was. I couldn't let him marry Bonita. She would have, all right, if I'd let her alone. The night before she was to marry the Judge, she ran off to Fargo's ranch. If he'd been home she'd have gone off with him, I guess, but when I got there she was alone. I took a buggy whip to her and fetched her to town."

"How'd you get her to marry the Judge?"

"I reasoned with her," Ivor said. "I told her the old man couldn't live long and when he died, she'd get everything he owned. I said Fargo would wait for her if he loved her, and then she could marry him and make him rich. He wouldn't have to go on robbing banks and whatever he was doing. I guess she married the old goat thinking she'd kill him herself someday. I reckon she's had reason enough since then to do it."

He frowned and looked away from Clint. "I dunno.

Mebbe I was wrong. Last time I was in town she wouldn't even see me."

"Think she'll run off with Fargo if he shows up?"

"She might. She's plain foolish some ways. She'd have to be to have fallen in love with that bastard in the first place, but I've been hoping she'd be over it by now."

"Maybe she is," Clint said. "Any strangers been across the bridge since Monday noon?"

"Nope. I ain't seen much of nobody except Mickey Shawn who's been out here three times since that telegraph line went down. But I'll tell you something that's damned funny. There's a couple of strangers on the other side of the river. I've seen 'em up on the rim yonder looking down at me. Or the bridge. Whatever they was looking at was mighty interesting to 'em."

"Sure you didn't know either one?"

"Neither one was Fargo, if that's what you're thinking."

"But you're sure they're strangers?"

"No, I ain't," Ivor admitted. "I've watched 'em through my glasses and I think one of 'em is that Happy Reese who used to hang around the Gay Lady mooching drinks. I just ain't sure. The other one I never seen before."

Clint turned to his horse. "Unlock the gate," he said. "I'm going across."

"You can't, Clint," Ivor said. "It's my guess they're the ones who have been cutting the wire. If they're still around, they'll plug you."

"Maybe, but I've got to find out. Somebody in town is playing on Fargo's side. I want to know who it is. Might be these fellows know." Clint stepped into the saddle. "Go on. Open up the gate."

"Damn it, you ain't got no authority on that side of the river. It's in another county."

"If I find 'em, I'll show 'em my authority, which is

the smoke end of my six-shooter. Now will you open that gate?''

''If you're bound to commit suicide, I reckon I can't stop you,'' Ivor muttered, and walking to the gate, unlocked and opened it.

Clint rode across the bridge, glancing down at the swirling water below him. Then he was on the other side, the north wall of the canyon rising directly above him. Bill Ivor could be right about him committing suicide, but a man didn't take a deputy's star because the job was a safe one.

He tried not to think of Nan, but he couldn't keep her out of his mind. Suddenly he wished he had married her; he knew he had been wrong in putting her off. They could at least have had a little time together. Now they might not have any.

Ten

THE ROAD FOLLOWED THE RIVER FOR THE FIRST HALF MILE BEYOND the toll bridge, forming a shelf so narrow that Clint wondered how a stagecoach or freight wagon could stay on it. The road had been hacked out of the red sandstone, the wall to Clint's right rising more than one hundred feet straight up from the river before it sloped back toward the slickrock rim far above the stream.

The question in Clint's mind was not why it wasn't wider, but how the builders had managed to make it as wide as it was. The telegraph wires ran along the bank between the road and the river, most of the poles propped upright by piles of rock. Now and then one of the poles leaned precariously over the water. The line for this half mile at least would be difficult to keep up, and it was understandable that on occasion the wires would be down. But this time they had been down too long for it to be an accident.

An army of men could hide on the slope above Clint

and he wouldn't be able to see them from the road. On the other hand, they couldn't see him, but that was small comfort. If the two men Bill Ivor had mentioned were watching the toll bridge, they certainly had seen Clint cross the river and they'd be watching for him.

Half a mile from the bridge a creek entered the river from the right, cutting a gash into the side of the cliff. At this point there were several acres of level ground. Here the road continued to run along the bank of the river until it nearly reached the creek, and then swung north in a loop. Both the road and the telegraph line used the side canyon to reach the top, swinging back and forth across the creek to cut down the grade.

When Clint reached the junction of the two streams, he saw that the wires were down, their ends trailing in the water. His first impulse was to dismount and take a look at the wires to see if they had been cut, but he realized immediately that if he did he would be far enough out on the level ground to come into view of the men if they were watching. He was convinced that this was the reason they had chosen this particular place to cut the wires.

If a crew of linemen came out from Grand Junction to repair the break, the men on the cliff would simply wait until they left, then come down and cut the wires again. But a lawman would be something else. Any friend of Ben Fargo would try to kill him. The chances were they had recognized Clint when he crossed the bridge. Happy Reese certainly would, if Bill Ivor was right about him being one of them.

Reese was a no-good saddle bum. Clint had thrown him into jail more than once for being drunk and disorderly, always wondering where the fellow got enough money to get drunk on. He seldom worked, although Clint remembered that he used to give Ben Fargo a hand at branding time. He was, Clint judged, a man who never refused a chance to earn a dishonest dollar, although he wasn't a bad one in the sense that Ben Fargo and Duke were.

Clint made a quick decision, and, reining over close to the cliff, jerked his rifle from the boot and dismounted. He didn't have much time, but for a few minutes at least the hidden men would probably watch the cut wires, expecting him to show himself at that point. If Bill Ivor hadn't warned him, that's exactly what he would have done. Now he had to find out if they were really up there, or if he was jumping at shadows.

He began climbing, keeping low and crowding the bank on his right. His greatest fear was that he would kick up enough dust to give himself away, so he stayed on the rocks except where he had to cross the edge of one of the switchbacks. In spite of his caution, he apparently lifted enough dust to be seen, or possibly he hadn't kept low enough and one of them had glimpsed the top of his hat.

The sharp crack of a rifle knifed into the stillness. The bullet went over Clint's head by a good three feet. He leaped up and fell forward, his hands flung out as if he had been hard hit, then scrambled on up the slope through a nest of boulders.

One of the men yelled jubilantly, "You got him, Happy. The way he fell you must have got him right through the brisket."

When he was ten feet above the place where he had fallen, Clint straightened up, his rifle on the ready. The man who had yelled called again, "Come on, Happy." He was running toward the place where Clint had gone down. Suddenly he saw Clint and instinctively dived toward a nearby ledge.

He never made it. Clint's bullet caught him in midair; it knocked him flat and he started rolling toward the river. He clawed frantically at a small cedar and missed; he succeeded in grabbing a rock that was loosely imbedded in the shallow soil, but it gave way. Now there was nothing to stop him and he went over the edge, a small rock slide going with him. If the bullet hadn't killed him, the drop of more than one hundred feet certainly would.

Clint had not forgotten the other man. He dropped belly flat, his eyes searching the slope for the fellow. He caught no hint of movement; he heard nothing except the pound of the river below him. Then a battered black hat was lifted on a stick above a ledge, and a man shouted, "Harper, can you hear me?"

"Yeah, I can hear you."

"I'm Happy Reese. I'm the one who shot at you. I wasn't trying to hit you. I just wanted to warn you. I wouldn't have got into this if I'd knowed there was gonna be any shooting."

"Stand up. Get your hands in the air."

Reese obeyed, calling shrilly, "Don't shoot me, Harper. I saved your life just now. I could have killed you if I'd aimed to."

Clint doubted that, but there was no point in arguing as long as Reese was surrendering. Clint asked, "Where's your horses?"

"Yonder." Reese motioned with an arm. "Back of that boulder."

"Get 'em," Clint said, knowing the man wouldn't attempt a fast ride to escape on a slope like this, caught between the slickrock rim above him and the cliff next to the river below him.

As Clint watched Reese walk to the boulder and disappear behind it, he told himself that Happy Reese was a coward and the other man had been a fool to expose himself the way he had. Then he thought sourly that this was only the beginning, that Ben Fargo had been forced to use whoever he could, and that the situation would get worse before it got better. Fargo was neither a fool nor a coward.

A few minutes later Reese reached the road leading two horses. Clint asked, "Who was your friend?"

"I don't know," Reese blurted, his shifty eyes fixing

on Clint's face for a moment, then turning away. "I reckon you'll think I'm lying, but by God, I ain't. I don't know nothing about him except that his first name is Muley. He hired me to help him cut the wires and keep 'em cut. Till tonight, that is, then we was done. He was gonna give me a hundred dollars."

"Did he say why he wanted 'em cut?"

"Yeah. Something about a big business deal and he didn't want no news coming into San Lorenzo till after sundown tonight. I figgered he was in cahoots with old Judge Wallace."

Reese might be lying again, but Clint had no time to stand here trying to worm the truth out of him. And there was a chance he wasn't lying. He was the kind who would do almost anything for that much whisky money.

"Mount up," Clint said. "You try making a run for it and you'll get a bullet in your back before you go ten feet."

"Not me," Reese said as he stepped into the saddle. "I don't figger on taking no chances like that."

"You know you'll go to the pen for cutting the wires?"

Reese nodded, his gaze touching Clint's face briefly. "Sure, but it's better'n hanging and it's better'n having a slug in my back. I've learned my lesson, Harper. When I get out of the pen, I'll get me a job."

Clint allowed himself a smile as he mounted the second horse. This time he knew Reese was lying. When they reached the river, he changed to his horse and turned upstream. A moment later he reached the man he had shot. He was lying at the edge of the road within a foot of the bank. If he had made one more turn, he would have fallen into the swift water and been carried downstream.

Clint turned him over on his back. He was dead. His face was scratched and battered, but Clint was sure he had never seen the man before. He lifted the body to the empty saddle and lashed it securely into place, then turned to Reese.

"I want to know who this bastard is," he said.

"Before God, I tell you I don't know," Reese cried, his face reflecting his terror.

Reese knew he wasn't being believed, Clint thought, and he expected to be shot. Again Clint decided that there was a chance Reese was telling the truth. Perhaps he was too scared to do anything else.

"How'd you get hooked up with him?" Clint asked.

Reese took a long breath. "Well, you know how it is with me. I ride the grub line and I ain't above taking a job like this if I get a chance. I used to help Ben Fargo some. He didn't work me hard and he always had plenty of whisky around. Since he got sent up, I've been holed up in his shack part of the time. I could usually shoot me a buck. Ben had a few steers around there and I'd kill one of them, thinking nobody would care."

Sweat ran down his face. He wiped a hand across it, not sure yet he was being believed. He hurried on, "I was in Ben's shack and I was getting mighty tired of eating nothing but meat. I was about out of shells and hadn't had a drink for a month when this Muley gent rides in. He made me an offer. Safe enough, he says. No killing. No big holdups or nothing, so I took it. We'd cut the wires, wait till they was fixed, then cut 'em again."

"You were watching the toll bridge?"

Reese nodded. "Most of the time. He kept saying that you or Ludlow would come out to see about it. We seen Bill Ivor working in his garden and such, and we seen Mickey Shawn ride out, but you'n Ludlow was the only ones Muley worried about."

Clint let it go at that, not knowing how much of what Reese had said was the truth. When they reached the toll bridge, Bill Ivor had the gate open for them. He looked at Reese, his mouth curling in distaste. "Glad to see you made it back, Clint, but sorry you didn't plug the varmit. Reckon he ain't worth a bullet, though. It'd be just as well to cut his throat."

"Maybe I will when I get him to town," Clint said. "He took a shot at me and missed on purpose, he claims. Says he saved my life."

Ivor snorted. "Hell, he'd save anybody's life he shot at." He walked to the dead man, took a handful of hair, and lifted his head so he could see his face. He let go and turned to Clint. "Muley Hanks. Used to ride with Duke Wade. I've seen him more'n once at Fargo's place. I heard he was with Wade at Trinidad when Wade got shot to pieces. Muley here got away."

Clint looked at Reese. "If that's the case, I'd say you'd seen this gent and knew who he was."

Ivor took a knife out of his pocket, opened it, and ran a finger along the edge of the blade. He said, "I ain't used this knife lately. I always kept it sharp to cut my pigs with. Why don't you leave Reese with me? No sense taking him to jail and wasting taxpayers' money feeding him. He just ain't worth it."

Reese let out a scared bleat. He said quickly, "Wait a minute, Harper. I lied a little bit. I knowed this hombre was Muley Hanks and I knowed he rode with Wade, but all he said was that Fargo was gonna make a try at busting out of the pen. If he made it, he wanted the wires cut so you'n Ludlow wouldn't hear about it."

"That's better," Clint said. "Now maybe you want to tell us who it is in town that's working with Fargo."

"I don't know that," Reese said quickly. "I'd tell you if I could, but I sure don't know."

Ivor replaced the knife. "Hanks was a fool. Never could be trusted to use his head to do a good job of anything, so maybe Fargo didn't want him told."

Clint nodded. "Might be. Well, I'll get Reese to jail."

"Wait a minute." Ivor walked to Reese's horse and

looked up, his hand dipping into his pocket and coming out with the knife again. "Which way is Fargo coming?"

Reese swallowed. Spit ran down his chin and he wiped it off with his sleeve. "The other way. That's all I know. All Hanks said was that we had to keep the wires cut till sundown tonight."

Ivor looked at Clint and shrugged. "How can you tell when this liar is telling the truth, if he ever does?"

"I can't," Clint said, "but it's my guess this is the truth. Doesn't make sense that Fargo would take the long way to get here."

"No, it don't," Ivor agreed. "Let me know if you hear anything different."

"I'll get word to you," Clint promised. "Let's ride, Reese."

When they reached town, Clint left Muley Hanks's body at Doc Julian's office and took Reese to the county jail and locked him up. Ludlow wasn't in the sheriff's office. Clint asked the county clerk about him, and the man said he hadn't seen Ludlow since early morning and hadn't heard anything about him.

Clint glanced at the clock on the wall. It was half-past one. Ludlow was in trouble or he'd have been back before now.

ELEVEN

MARGE RAINER RETURNED TO THE TABLE AFTER CLINT LEFT and finished kneading the bread. She worked mechanically, her mind on Bonita and the letters she had received from Ben Fargo. Then her thoughts turned to Tom Ludlow and herself. Now that it was too late, she knew she had been stupid to think she could keep the townspeople from knowing what she and Tom Ludlow had been doing.

Clint Harper was the best friend she had. Maybe the only real friend. She had to believe what he had said about Tom. Clint wouldn't lie. He had no reason to, and he certainly knew Tom inside and out. Still, knowing she should believe something and actually believing it were two different things.

The trouble was that she wanted to believe with all of her heart that Tom had meant what he'd said when he'd told her he loved her. She could not face the future and not believe in Tom, for all of her dreams and hopes were based on her love for him and his supposed love for her.

Now, although her conscious mind told her that Clint was right, that his words had destroyed her plans just as a morning sun burns away the night fog, she could not actually bring herself to give up the dreams that had meant so much to her.

She shaped the dough into loaves, placed them in pans, and set the pans on a pantry shelf to rise. Then she left the house and started up the hill toward Judge Wallace's house. She glanced back and saw that Shorty Bogardus was watching her. She wondered bitterly what lecherous thoughts were in his mind. Did all men have those thoughts when they looked at her?

She went on, walking fast. She had always liked Shorty and felt that he liked her. He often came over from the livery stable and cut wood for her or did some of the chores around the house that needed doing and were too heavy for her, chores that Tom Ludlow never saw.

She had thought that Shorty only wanted to be neighborly the same as Sam Calloway and some of the other men who had dropped around to see if they could help her. It had never occurred to her that they recognized her for what she was, that each was hoping she would break up with Ludlow so one of them could move in. But maybe she was being unfair to them, for none of them had indicated by word or gesture anything of the kind.

Clint had said that the women thought the worst of her and the men the best. Now, panting from the climb, she stopped to catch her breath and remembered how it had been when she'd first moved to town. The wives had combined against her to let her know she wasn't welcome. The Literary Society. The Ladies' Aid. Even the church had given her the cold shoulder.

This treatment as much as anything had driven her into Tom Ludlow's arms. She was not a woman who could live alone or even be alone for long periods of time. Because she was Clint's friend, Nan Carney had dropped in to see her occasionally, but she and Nan had never been close. She suspected that Nan's visits were duty calls made at Clint's suggestion.

She went on up the hill, thinking that Bonita was her only female friend, and that they had been drawn together because each was desperately lonely. But Bonita's friendship had not been enough. Marge needed to love and to be loved, and Tom Ludlow had been available. So she could blame the "good" women of the town for making her a "bad" woman. But the truth was it didn't do any good to blame someone else.

No one had forced her to become a wanton. She had done exactly what she had wanted to do, and she might as well face that hard fact. She could stay here and accept her reputation, or she could leave and go somewhere else and start over. As she stepped up on the Wallace porch and tugged at the bell pull, she wasn't sure which course she would choose.

Bonita opened the door and smiled when she saw who it was. "Marge, I'm glad to see you. It's been so long. Come in."

"It has been a long time," she said, and stepped inside. She knew that Bonita would not be glad to see her when she found out why she had come.

She followed Bonita into the parlor, which was filled with expensive furniture. The heavy blue drapes at the windows and the maroon portiers between the hall and the parlor combined with the furniture to give the room the subdued and melancholy atmosphere of a funeral home.

As she sat down, she sensed Bonita's bitterness. She couldn't blame the girl. Judge Wallace had never allowed her to share the position that he held in the community. She was not permitted to entertain her friends, or even to entertain in the way she wanted. Before the Judge had become bedfast he had on occasion invited guests for Sunday dinner, but it was always someone like Doug Carney and Nan, or Doc Julian and his wife, or perhaps some visiting dignitary the Judge wanted to impress. To the Judge his wife was a combination housekeeper and private plaything.

Bonita sat in a black leather rocking chair across the room from Marge. A stray gleam of sunshine falling through the open drapes touched her face. She looked far too old for her years, Marge thought. She nervously clasped her hands on her lap and dropped them to her sides and then clasped them on her lap again.

There was a moment of strained silence, and then Bonita asked with forced gaiety, "How's your romance with Tom Ludlow coming?"

Marge felt her face burn. "I guess everyone knows," she said. "I didn't think people did, but I was like the ostrich with his head in the sand. I get along fine with Tom as long as I entertain him the way he wants to be entertained."

"Well, I'd like a chance to entertain him that way," Bonita said. "It would be a relief after living with that old goat upstairs."

Marge had heard Bonita talk this way before, but it always shocked her. Bonita never seemed to feel any guilt for doing something wrong. Instead, she often gloried in it.

"How is the Judge?" Marge asked.

"Mean, the way he always is," Bonita said. "I'll bet he lives for ten years. I can't stand it that long. Pa made me marry him and he got a good job out of it, but look at what I got."

"What would you have done if you hadn't married the Judge?"

"Run off with Ben Fargo, I guess."

"And helped him rob banks and hold up stages?"

Bonita laughed. "Maybe I would have."

"And gone to Canon City with him."

The girl shrugged. "It would have been better than this. You don't know, Marge. You just don't know."

"No, I guess I don't," Marge admitted. "What will you do if Fargo does come back?"

"Do?" Bonita looked blank. "I won't do anything. Anyhow, he's in prison. He won't show up."

"Clint thinks he will. He'll want you to run off with him. Will you do it?"

"Of course not. I've grown up a little bit. Besides, I've got too much invested here to go off with an escaped convict. The Judge is going to die someday. When he does, I'll take his money and get out of town."

"But if Fargo does come and Clint and Tom can't protect you, you'll be in trouble. My husband and I knew Fargo when he was a boy. He was wicked, Bonita, the cruelest boy I ever knew. From what I've heard, he got worse as he got older. I'd guess that prison has made him still worse."

"It probably has," Bonita agreed, "but it's no concern of mine. I just won't go. I don't have any use for him any more. I'll tell him so."

"Then he'll use you and he'll kill you." Marge shifted her weight in the chair. "Bonita, Sam Calloway told Clint about the letters I'd been getting from Canon City and Clint came to me. I had to tell him they were for you."

Bonita's face turned white. She swore angrily, and then, filled with a fury that swept entirely out of control, screamed, "You promised you wouldn't. What kind of a friend are you?"

"I'm sorry I had to break my promise," Marge said, "but this is serious. I didn't have any choice. I know how bad Fargo is. So does Clint. He wants you to talk to him this afternoon. He's gone to the toll bridge. To warn your pa, I guess, but he said he'd be back by one and for you to come to my place."

"I won't do it," Bonita said shrilly. "It's my business about those letters. They aren't important anyhow. I haven't written to Ben for a long time. I haven't even heard from him for over two months. You tell Clint Harper he can go to hell."

"Then he'll come here," Marge said. "I told him I had promised not to tell about the letters and I didn't want to ask you to see him, but he said he had to talk to you. I think it would be less trouble all around if you came to my house."

Bonita opened her mouth, but before she could say more than "I won't . . . ," a bell rang from upstairs. She rose, frightened, Marge thought, because she was afraid she'd been speaking too loud and the Judge had heard what she'd said. "Excuse me, Marge. I've got to go when the King summons me."

She was back in a few minutes, her face pale. "I'll see Clint. I'll tell him anything I can." She swallowed, and then the bitterness and the hatred possessed her again, and she said slowly, "I hope Ben comes back and kills the Judge. I hope to God he does."

"You don't really hope that," Marge said gently. "I guess there are degrees of evil. What Tom and I have done is evil. The way you feel about the Judge and your pa is evil. But they're small evils when you compare them with what Ben Fargo will do when he comes to San Lorenzo."

Bonita began to cry. Marge put an arm around the girl, and hugged her. "It's good for you to cry," Marge said softly. "I've got a lot of crying to do, too."

She left the house and walked down the hill, but now, for some reason she didn't understand, the need to cry was gone. Instead, a sense of rebellion possessed her. If the people of San Lorenzo with their small, mean talk had condemned her as a bad woman, she might as well have the game as well as the name.

When she reached her house, she saw Shorty Bogardus

was pumping water into a horse trough back of his stable. She walked to him. He was making so much noise with the pump that he didn't know she was there until she put a hand on his shoulder. He jumped and whirled, and backed away, embarrassed.

"I'm out of wood, Shorty," she said. "If you have time. . . ."

"Glad to Marge," he said. "I've got plenty of time. Nothing but time, far as that goes."

"I'll heat the coffee up," she said, "I've got a chocolate cake that I think you'll like."

"Sure I'll like it. I never et one of your cakes that I didn't."

She stayed in the kitchen while he chopped wood. When the coffee was hot, she called him into the house. She cut a big slab of cake and poured a cup of coffee for him. She sat down, her chair close to his, a cup in her hand, and she saw that the intimacy of the moment bothered him. When he had finished eating, he rose and thanked her.

"It's a small thing to do, Shorty," she said, "compared to cutting the wood. I'm so grateful to you."

"I'd do anything for you," Shorty said. "You know I would."

He left then. She stood by the door watching him as he crossed the vacant lot toward his stable. She felt an inner peace that was a welcome relief from the turmoil that had been in her since she had opened the door that morning to Clint Harper's knock. She had not been sure what Clint had meant by saying the men thought the best of her. There were two ways she could take it, a bad and a good way, but now she was sure he had meant it the good way. Shorty respected her and perhaps Tom Ludlow, in spite of his fine talk, never had.

In that moment she made up her mind. There would be no more favors for Tom until their marriage night. The next time she saw him, she would tell him so.

She cooked her dinner and ate, then washed and dried the dishes. She walked through the house, trying to think of something to do, but she could not. She sat down by a window to wait for Bonita and Clint, depressed by her loneliness. By half past one neither had come.

Twelve

When Clint had ridden into town his mind had been so firmly fixed on delivering Muley Hanks's body to Doc Julian and jailing Happy Reese that he had not noticed anything unusual about Main Street. Now, as he left the courthouse, it suddenly struck him that no one was in sight. There wasn't even a saddle horse or team and rig tied to the hitch poles that lined the short street of the business block.

He paused in front of Mom Risdon's café. Ordinarily a few businessmen would be coming back from a late dinner at this time; a housewife would be going into Sam Calloway's store or leaving it. Even in the middle of the week, as it was now, there would normally be a few horses and teams on the street.

Clint had the weird feeling he was standing on Main Street of a deserted town. Some of the stores and offices actually had their shades drawn. Probably the doors were locked. The only signs of life were two Plymouth Rock hens dusting themselves at the edge of the street in front of Shorty Bogardus' livery stable, and a yellow dog dozing on the walk at the corner of Sam Calloway's store.

A chill traveled down Clint's spine as he turned into the café, for this was a new and strange feeling, as if San Lorenzo had become a town of ghosts within a matter of hours. The townspeople had got the word that Fargo was coming, so some of them had gone home and probably locked their doors, businessmen who normally would never be gone from their stores or offices at this time of day except on Sunday, a legal holiday, or during a funeral of a prominent person in the community. Before dark fear would turn to panic and many of them would leave.

Clint sat down on a stool at the counter and called, "Mom."

She came out of the kitchen, her face flushed from bending over the hot stove. "Howdy, Clint. Didn't hear you come in. If I had, I'd have been too scared to show my face till I heard you holler."

"Looks like the whole town's scared," he said. "Far as I could see, the population consists of one dog and two hens."

"That's about it. Clint, all of us who heard Fargo's threats have been living scared ever since. We didn't need to hear nothing except that he was coming."

Clint shrugged. "He didn't say he was going to wipe the town out." He nodded at the kitchen. "What can you fetch me pronto?"

"I've got a ham," she said. "Just take a minute to slice it."

"That'll do."

She disappeared into the kitchen and returned a moment later with a plate heaped with sliced ham and boiled potatoes. She brought coffee, bread, and butter, then stood in front of him, her fat arms folded across her chest.

She was a pushy woman, loud of voice, with huge

breasts and a tongue dripping with vicious gossip. Clint thoroughly disliked her because she was largely responsible for cutting Marge Rainer's throat socially when Marge moved to town. The odd part of it was that she had no need to worry about losing her husband to a seductive widow. Lafe Risdon was a small, docile man who "enjoyed" poor health and seldom left the house.

"Clint," she began, "I hear that Fargo will ride into town before dark with fifty cutthroats and they'll burn the town and kill every one of us. Is that true?"

"No."

"How do you know?"

"He couldn't find fifty men."

"Well." She glared at him. "Now that's mighty peculiar figuring. Of course he could find fifty men if he promised them enough loot and women they could rape."

He wanted to tell her she'd be safe, but he restrained himself. Instead, he said, "We'll have to form a posse and go meet Fargo. If Lafe's here, let me talk to him."

"Lafe's home," she snapped. "You know he's sickly."

"That's no excuse," Clint said. "When Tom Ludlow gets back, we'll have to draft every man in town. Lafe wouldn't want you raped and the town burned."

She glared at him, her face redder than ever. She said, "Lafe don't have good eyes. He can't see to shoot straight. It's up to you and Tom Ludlow to protect the town."

"Tom's gone," Clint said.

"Then it's up to you," she said, and whirled and stomped back to the kitchen.

Clint grinned wryly. At least he could finish his meal in silence. When he was done, he dropped a coin on the counter and left the café. As he hurried to Marge's house, he saw that the street was still deserted. Not that he had expected anything else. There would be no change until Fargo was gone.

Resentment grew in him as he thought about Mom Risdon saying it was up to him and Tom Ludlow to protect the town. Judge Wallace, on the other hand, would say it was up to them to protect him. His thoughts turned to Ludlow. The sheriff should have been back two hours ago. It was quite possible that he wasn't in trouble at all, but had decided that the best way to stay alive was to keep on riding.

By the time Clint reached Marge's house, he was close to the boiling point. It was bad enough to have some of the businessmen lock up and go home. To have the sheriff ride out and leave the job to him was too much. Still, he should have expected both to happen.

Marge saw him coming, and called from her back porch, "Clint, Bonita hasn't come."

This threw more fuel on the fire of Clint's temper. He should have expected it, too. Any woman who had been fool enough to write to Ben Fargo wouldn't want to talk about it or even admit it. Without a word he went on, swinging around the house to the street in front.

"Wait, Clint." Marge ran after him. "Can't you come in for a minute?"

He turned. "No. If Bonita doesn't want to come, I'll go to her." Then he realized he might be jumping to the wrong conclusion. Marge might not even have told Bonita to be here. "You saw Bonita?"

Marge nodded. "I saw her all right. She had a fit. Said I had no business telling you about it. I knew she'd be mad. At first she said she wouldn't come, then the Judge must have heard her screaming at me. She was yelling loud enough. Anyway, he rang the bell and she went upstairs to him. When she came back, she was scared and kind of trembly. She said she'd see you and tell you anything you wanted to know."

"You haven't seen her since?"

"No, and I'm worried. It isn't like her to break a promise."

"She didn't tell you what the Judge said?"

"No, but after she told me she'd see you, I'll swear she looked like the devil had hold of her. You know how she gets sometimes, all filled up with hating the Judge. She was that way, only worse. She said she hoped Fargo would come back and kill the Judge."

He nodded. This was something he could understand. It was possible the Judge would drive her to the place where she would kill him herself.

"I'll go up there and see," he said.

"Clint," Marge said, her gaze on the ground, "have you seen Tom?"

"Not since morning. He went to warn Matt Smith. I've got a hunch he just kept riding."

"Clint, he wouldn't." She looked directly at him, indignant at this accusation of cowardice. "Maybe Tom isn't all he should be, but he wouldn't do that."

He sensed her misery, but he wasn't sorry he had said what he had. She needed a jolt. He said, "Remember one thing, Marge. You've always seen his best side. I've seen the other side."

He went on, climbing the hill to the Wallace house. The thought occurred to him that there were times when good came out of evil. If this Fargo mess cured Marge of her love for Tom Ludlow, it would be one worth-while thing.

Clint didn't know what to expect when he yanked the bell pull of the Wallace house, but a sense of urgency prodded him. One tragedy could lead to another. Just the threat of Fargo's return had upended Pandora's box of evil upon the town. If Fargo never showed up, he had already taken a healthy revenge upon those he hated.

When Clint tugged on the bell pull a second time and it went unanswered, he opened the door and walked in.

No one was in the parlor. He heard Wallace yell something from his room. At least he was still alive.

Clint continued his search for Bonita, ignoring Wallace's yells and the ringing of his bell. When Clint was certain that Bonita was not in any of the rooms on the first floor, he climbed the stairs to Wallace's bedroom.

The old man had worked himself into a fury, knowing that whoever was in the house had completely ignored his calls. He was sitting on the edge of the bed, his white nightgown hiked up to his knees.

The old man was trembling, sweat running down his face. Clint was shocked when he looked at Wallace's legs, mere pipestems compared to what they once had been, the skin clinging tightly to the bone. They wouldn't carry him halfway across the room. For the first time in his life, Clint felt a flash of sympathy for this imperious old man who had imposed his will on so many, and now was dependent for his very life upon someone else.

Wallace wiped a sleeve across his face. He glared at Clint, his eyes as predatory as those of a great eagle. He tried to shout, but his voice came out thin and reedy. "So it's you who's walking through my house as if you owned it. What the hell are you doing here?"

"Trying to find Bonita."

"She's not here. I don't know where she went. I'll fix her when she gets back, going off and leaving me like this." He lifted his legs back into bed with an effort, his gaze fixed on Clint's face. "What do you want with her?"

"My business."

"Bonita's business is my business," Wallace said angrily. "You'd better tell me. If I think you're smelling around after my wife because I'm old and she's young, I'll kill you."

"You're the dirtiest-minded old booger I ever saw," Clint said in disgust.

He left the room and searched the upstairs for the girl.

Wallace was right. She wasn't in the house. Returning to the Judge's room, he said, "I don't know when Fargo's going to get here, but he'll show up sooner or later. Tom Ludlow's gone. He should have been back two or three hours ago. I need help and there's no one in town I can count on except maybe Sam Calloway."

Wallace waggled a talonlike finger at Clint, "I want protection. I told you that this morning. If Ludlow's gone, it's up to you to keep that murdering bastard away from me."

"I've got too much to do to wet nurse you," Clint said sharply. "You need protection, all right, but you've got to furnish it yourself. I stopped at the Box W this morning and asked Irish O'Brien to send some men to town, but he wouldn't do it because you hadn't given him the order. Now you'd better do it pronto. Send Andy Downs out there with a note."

Wallace shook his head. "You and Ludlow are paid to enforce the law. You earn your pay and Irish and the Box W crew will earn theirs."

"Then you'd better savvy this," Clint said. "If the town is destroyed and the people killed, you'll be to blame because you've got the men to prevent it."

"Don't put the blame on me," Wallace snapped. "Looks to me like you're not qualified to carry that star. You're fired."

Clint laughed. "You're not only pigheaded. You're stupid in everything except making money. You can't fire me. It'll have to be Ludlow."

"We'll see, we'll see."

"I think we will," Clint agreed. "There's another thing. If Fargo comes from the west, he'll cross the toll bridge and he'll kill Bill Ivor. I tried to get Bill to come to town, but he said you'd fire him. Now you send Andy out there with orders for Bill to come in, or his blood will be on your head, too."

"Bill Ivor can look out for himself." Wallace lay back on the pillow, his strength gone. "Find Bonita for me, Harper. Send her up here."

"Then you won't give me any help?" Clint asked.

"No, by God, I won't."

Clint stared at the old, wrinkled face. Only the eyes held the familiar spark of imperious authority that had always been so much a part of the man. He might be dying, but he wouldn't change.

There was an end to arguing with arrogance and stubbornness, and Clint had reached it. Without another word he turned and left the room. He went down the stairs and out of the house. Andy Downs was not in sight. Judge Wallace was more alone than he had ever been before in his life.

Clint glanced at his watch. It was twenty-five minutes after two.

THIRTEEN

ALL CLINT COULD DO WAS WAIT. HE HAD ASSUMED FROM the beginning that Fargo would not make his appearance until after dark. What Reese had said about being hired to keep the wires cut until sundown bore out that assumption.

He returned to the sheriff's office to see if Ludlow had come in. The sheriff wasn't there, but Bonita was. She said sullenly, "Marge says you wanted to see me."

"Yes, I want to see you." Clint sat down in Ludlow's chair and slammed his hat on the desk. "I told Marge to have you come to her house."

Bonita stood by a west window, the afternoon sun touching her with harsh brightness. Now she turned so her back was to the window, her gaze on Clint, her hands clenched at her sides. She was silent, her breasts rising and falling with her breathing. She was, he thought, the most strikingly beautiful woman he had ever seen: in the dark and vivid coloring of her skin, the regularity of her features, the perfection of her figure. Yet something was lacking.

Leaning back in his chair, his eyes meeting hers, he told himself that beauty was more than the superficial things a man saw with his eyes. Bonita had everything, yet it was nothing. She had been unable to accept her life, so she had permitted her serenity of spirit to be marred by hatred and bitterness and resentment. Here was the difference between her and Nan, who had ample reason to hate her father for his futility and selfish indifference to her happiness. But she hadn't, and so, to Clint, she was a more desirable woman than Bonita.

"Well, what do you want?" Bonita demanded after a long pause.

"You know," Clint said. "Your writing to Ben Fargo. Tell me about it."

"Yes, I know, all right," she admitted. "I guess that was why I didn't go to Marge's house. I was foolish to write to Ben in the first place, and more foolish to keep it up after I knew it was wrong, but you've got to believe one thing. I don't want to have anything to do with Ben Fargo now or any time."

"You may have a hard time convincing him of that when he gets here," Clint said.

"I know," she said, "and I'm scared. More scared than I ever was in my life before. After Marge left this morning, I started to walk. That's what I've been doing ever since. I finally decided to see you because I was scared. I'm not going back to the Judge's house because Ben would expect to find me there, but I don't know where I can go that would be safe."

"We'll figure something out," Clint said. "I'd like to see Fargo's letters."

"I burned them six months ago," she said. "The ones he wrote since then I burned as soon as I got them. I started writing to him when he first went to prison. I told him to write to Marge and I'd get them from her. I did it because I was mad at Pa for making me marry the Judge and I was mad at the Judge. You know the kind of life I've had in that tomb of a house. It took a while, but I finally figured out that I'd be worse off married to Ben. I didn't ever love him. I was young and crazy enough to admire his kind of life. Living down there the way we did, well, I guess I thought anything would be better."

She crossed the room and sat down in front of the desk. "I'm not proud of myself, Clint, but the Judge never tried to make me love him. Sure, he dressed me up and showed me off and bragged about me being pretty, but I was never more than a housekeeper. Once he called me a halfbreed and said he was ashamed of me. I don't know whether he ever loved either one of his first wives or not, but I doubt it. I don't think he knows what it is to love anything."

She moistened her lips with the tip of her tongue, then went on, "After a while I saw he wasn't going to live much longer, and I decided I wasn't going to throw away a fortune, so I wrote to Ben and told him to quit writing. He got mad and wrote three more letters. The last one came two months ago, but he never said anything about breaking out of prison."

"Did he ever say who was his friend here in town?" Clint asked. "Who was going to help him when he came back?"

She shook her head. "No. He always said he expected me to go away with him when he came and that he was going to collect some old debts, but that was all."

Clint leaned back in his chair and rolled a cigarette. He'd had a thin hope that he might find some clue in Fargo's letters to the identity of the man in San Lorenzo who had written those three words on the livery stable door.

That man, whoever he was, was the key to what would happen when Fargo got here. He could hide Fargo so the man could strike when and where he wanted; he would give Fargo food, a gun, shells, a fresh horse when the blood bath was over. If Clint could read those letters . . .

"Bonita, are you lying to me?" he demanded. "Did you really burn those letters?"

"I'm not lying," she said indifferently. "I don't care what you think, but I don't want you going around telling about me and Ben writing to each other. If the Judge heard it, he'd throw me out and change his will."

"I'm not going to tell anyone," Clint said. "Nobody knows but Marge."

"She said Sam Calloway told you."

Clint shook his head. "He thinks Fargo was writing to Marge. Now you've got to go home. The Judge doesn't know what happened to you. I didn't see Andy Downs around there. Somebody's got to look out for the old man. I didn't realize how much he'd failed until I saw him today."

"I can't, Clint. I tell you that's the first place Fargo would look for me. What do you think he'd do if he found me?"

"You'd go with him or he'd kill you," Clint said, "but we've got five or six hours, I think. Maybe more. See if you can get the Judge to send Andy to the Box W for help. Tell him you won't stay in the house without protection."

"I'll try," she said, "but it won't do any good. I've never got him to change his mind about anything. You saw how it was this morning."

"He was the same this afternoon," Clint said, "but it's the only chance we've . . ."

A running man's boots hammered on the hall floor. Clint whirled in the swivel chair as Shorty Bogardus burst into the room. He was as frightened as when he'd got Clint out of bed that morning. "Sure glad . . ." He stopped and sucked in a long, panting breath. "I found you. Come on."

"Come on where?"

"Hurry up." Shorty jerked his head at the door. "Get up out of that chair and come on."

"What's the matter with you?"

"He's here, that's what. Will you come on?"

"Who's here?"

"Fargo, damn it. Can't you get nothing through your solid bone head?"

Clint picked up his hat and rose. He checked his gun, took three long steps toward the door, then stopped. "Where is he? Did you see him?"

"No. I'd be dead if I had. But there's another note on my barn door. The back one this time. Just says, 'Fargo is here.' That's enough, ain't it?"

"Maybe," Clint said. "Maybe not. Whoever did the writing is trying to scare us. Nothing would do the job as well as getting the notion into our heads that Fargo has sneaked into town and is just waiting for his chance to start cracking some caps."

"Well, come on and look at it," Shorty said. "Maybe the bastard wrote it himself. Maybe he's hiding in my barn right now and laughing up his sleeve at me. I tell you, Clint, I've got a notion to saddle up a horse and get out of this here town till you get him."

"Till *I* get him?" Clint stared at the little liveryman. "I'm getting right down tired of hearing that. I can ride, too, you know."

They left the courthouse, Bonita following. They reached the San Lorenzo House before the thought struck Clint that Shorty had inadvertently pointed out the reason for the writing which on the face of it seemed childish and foolish. This had been planned by someone, not just to frighten folks for Fargo's enjoyment as Clint had been assuming, but to scare most of the townspeople out of San Lorenzo.

Clint turned this over in his mind as they walked through

the archway of the stable and along the runway to the back door. Who and what was Fargo after? Probably not all of the jurymen, but certainly Judge Wallace and Ludlow. Fargo would likely want him, too, Clint thought, for their enmity had gone back too far and was too deep to be ignored. And he'd rob the bank, of course.

Fargo would think he could count on these three men staying in town, and certainly no one would take the bank's money out of the safe. So Fargo would figure it would be easier to do what he came for if the town was nearly deserted than if he rode into San Lorenzo and had to fight fifteen or twenty men patrolling the streets with rifles. What he didn't know, Clint thought grimly, was the bitter fact that there weren't fifteen or twenty men who had the guts to do any patrolling. Most of them were already at home sitting behind locked doors.

Three men were in the back of the stable: Doc Julian, Sam Calloway, and Peter Larson from the Gay Lady. They nodded at him and he nodded back, then he glanced at the writing on the door. It was the same scrawl he had seen on the front door early that morning. Very likely it had been disguised, for it looked more like the writing of a small boy than a man, but Clint had long ago given up the hope that the whole thing was a kid's prank.

Then the thought struck Clint that most people didn't have chalk. It could be bought in Calloway's store, but it seemed improbable that anyone who had this business in mind would buy it. Calloway would remember. It was more likely to have come from the school. This pointed to the principal, Kenneth Delong, or one of the teachers. None of them, Clint decided, could be taken seriously. Some child must have slipped a piece into his pocket and taken it home and left it.

He wasn't much of a detective, he told himself ruefully, and turned to Sam Calloway. "Can you remember anyone who bought chalk in your store lately?"

"No," Calloway said.

"Shorty, you must know who's been in the stable since morning."

"It wasn't nobody who came in while I was here," Shorty said. "I'd taken me a nap after dinner. The way I sleep, some booger could have ridden a horse in here, done the writing, and rode out again."

"You said while you were here," Clint said. "Then you were out sometime?"

"Well . . . this morning . . ." Shorty's face turned red. "I cut a little wood for Marge. Somebody could have come in then."

"Any of you see a man come in this morning while Shorty was gone?" Clint asked.

They shook their heads. It seemed to Clint that all three looked guilty as if they were holding something back. He glanced at his watch. It was ten minutes till three. He had intended to speak to Delong about Danny Tebo and had forgotten all about it.

"I've got to get over to the school," Clint said. "After that I'll be in the sheriff's office or on the street if anyone wants me." He nodded at Bonita. "You'd better go on home. Main Street is no place for a woman."

"It sure ain't," Calloway said. "Ain't safe for nobody, looks to me."

Calloway walked out of the stable with Clint. As they passed through the archway, Calloway glanced back, saw that none of the others had followed and said in a low tone, "I didn't want to mention this in front of him, but I saw Doc Julian come out of the stable this morning."

Clint grinned. "I can't think of a poorer suspect."

"Neither can I," Calloway said, "but I thought I'd mention it."

He turned and crossed the street to his store. A moment later Doc Julian caught up with Clint, panting from his short run. He said, "I feel like a tattletale kid in school, but I saw Sam Calloway go into the stable after dinner. Shorty must have been asleep. I didn't want to say anything in front of Sam, but it did seem to me you ought to know."

Clint had trouble keeping a straight face. "Thanks, Doc, but I don't figure Sam's our man."

"Neither do I," Julian said, "but in a situation like this, you begin to suspect your own grandmother. I'm just as scared as the next man. I never told you or Ludlow, but before Fargo was arrested, he came to town one night and threw a gun on me and made me go to that stinking little ranch of his that never was anything but a robber's roost. One of Duke Wade's men had a bullet in him, and I had to take it out. The man died and Fargo was going to kill me. I think he would have if Wade hadn't talked him out of it."

Clint nodded. "You know, Doc, it's a funny thing, but when you start counting noses, Ben Fargo had reason to hate just about every man in this town."

"That's right," Julian agreed. "I never knew a man who seemed to thrive on hate the way he did. Well, I've got to hike over to Delong's place. She's about to have her baby and I promised to look in this afternoon."

Clint had not noticed Pete Larson who had loitered in front of the saloon while he tried to light a cigar but apparently had trouble keeping his match going. Now that Clint was alone, the saloon man slipped the cigar into his pocket and caught up with him. He said, "I didn't think it was right to speak up in front of the others, but Doug Carney was in the stable this morning. He dropped in for a drink after he left the stable, then he went to the bank."

"Thanks, Pete," Clint said, and strode on down the street.

He grinned wryly. This had become ridiculous. Doc Julian. Sam Calloway. Doug Carney. He could not think of three men in San Lorenzo who would be less likely to be involved with Ben Fargo.

FOURTEEN

THE SCHOOL PRINCIPAL, KENNETH DELONG, AD LIVED in San Lorenzo less than a year. Although he had heard about Ben Fargo and his threats, he had said repeatedly there was nothing to worry about, that if the man did break out of prison, he'd try to leave the state as soon as possible and not bother with getting revenge on the people who had convicted him.

So, when he answered Clint's knock on his door and stepped into the hall, he was highly irritated when he saw who it was. He shut the door behind him and said in a low voice, "Deputy, you won't get any place trying to shut down the school because of the absurd rumors I've been hearing all day. Any sane man would know there was nothing to this report about Ben Fargo coming back. I don't have time to argue the matter with you."

He would have gone back into the room if Clint hadn't put a foot against the door. He said mildly, "Perhaps you'd like to argue with a corpse I delivered to Doc Julian an hour or so ago. Or maybe with a prisoner named Happy Reese I locked up in jail."

"What are you talking about?"

"Reese and another man named Muley Hanks were hired to keep the wires cut between here and Grand Junction until tonight. Reese was told that Fargo was going to try to make a break. They took a shot at me and I killed Hanks and brought Reese in."

Delong was shocked, but he quickly recovered. "I still don't see what it has to do with me or the school. Fargo couldn't possibly have any interest in me or any of the children . . ."

"That's where you're wrong," Clint said. "Now get down off your high horse and listen to me. One of the men on the jury who convicted Fargo was Dan Tebo. He's dead, but his boy Danny is here. Fargo might decide . . ."

"Ridiculous," Delong snapped. "The boy had nothing to do with the trial."

"I haven't got time to argue with you, either," Clint said. "I want you to relieve Mrs. Tebo. I don't care what you do with the other kids, but have Mrs. Tebo and Danny get out of town for the night. She has friends among the ranchers where she can stay."

"I won't hear of it, Harper. You're scared. That's all. You're afraid of your shadow."

"I'm glad we have one brave man in town," Clint said. "I'll need you to patrol the streets as soon as it's dark and report to me when Fargo shows up."

This was something Delong had not expected. He swallowed with an effort, then said, "I'm sorry. I'll have to stay home. You know my wife's having a baby."

Clint grinned as he withdrew his foot from the door. Red-faced, Delong hurried back into the classroom. Clint's grin faded as he walked down the hall to Mrs. Tebo's room. Delong was probably the only man in San Lorenzo who saw little danger in Ben Fargo's return, but he was no different from the others when it came to giving help. Perhaps it was just as well, Clint thought. He'd likely shoot the wrong man anyhow.

Clint had no better luck with Mrs. Tebo when she came to the door. "You've heard about Fargo?" Clint asked, and she nodded. He said, "I've talked to Delong hoping I could get you and Danny out of town now, but he says no. What I want you to do is to get a rig from Shorty Bogardus and leave as soon as school's out. Take Danny and stay overnight. The Hectors are friends of yours. I'm sure they'll keep Danny until this is over with."

"You're pretty highhanded, Mr. Harper," she said. "I won't do anything of the kind."

"You can risk your life if you want to," Clint said, "but you have no right to risk Danny's. You don't seem to understand the kind of man Ben Fargo is."

"I understand perfectly. If my husband was alive, I'd be concerned, but he's beyond Fargo's reach. I have an engagement in town tonight, and I intend to keep it."

"What about Danny?"

"He'll be in the house. He'll be quite safe, I assure you. Nan mentioned this when she came this morning, but I simply refuse to get panicky about it. Now if you'll excuse me I'll go back to my children."

He swung around and left the building, then stopped and turned back. He couldn't let his anger at Delong's and Mrs. Tebo's stupidity get the best of him. It was possible Nan could do something. She came to the door when he knocked, and when she saw who it was, she stepped into the hall and moved away from the door so her students couldn't see her through the glass. She put her arms around Clint's neck and brought his face down for her kiss.

"It's been a long time since I kissed you," she said. "Eight-thirty this morning."

"It sure has," he agreed. "I guess you're about the only sane person left in town. Half of the businessmen on

Main Street have locked up and pulled the shades and gone home."

"I heard that," she said, "I guess Fargo is accomplishing what he wanted."

Clint nodded. "Most of them will be out of town by dark. Well, I'm not worried about the men who were on the jury. They've been warned and they can look out for themselves. Danny Tebo can't. I am worried about him, but neither Delong nor Mrs. Tebo will pay any attention."

"I know," she said. "I've talked to them."

"They may be right, but it's foolish to take any chances. I thought you might have an idea."

"I have," she said. "I was going to do it anyhow. Danny comes over in the evening once in a while and cuts wood for us. I'll have him tonight and he can stay for supper, but I don't know what to do after that. With Dad home, Danny might be in more danger in our house than if he were home."

Clint considered it a moment, then he said, "How would it be to get a rig and take him to the Hectors' place? It's not far from town and you could be back before dark. Or stay out there if you'd feel better."

"No, I wouldn't leave Dad alone, but I'll take Danny out there," she said.

"Good. I'll be on the move around town as soon as it's dark. I'll drop in on you just to check up."

"I wish you would," she said. "Clint, I'm scared."

"So am I," he said.

He left the building, and when he was back on Main Street, he saw that it was as deserted as it had been earlier in the afternoon. He paused in front of the bank, his gaze moving from one building to another. For a moment he had the terrifying thought that Delong was right, that he was scared of his shadow.

He could not remember having been really afraid of anything before in his life and he had faced physical danger of one kind or another many times. But this was different from anything he had ever been up against, partly because of the absolute animal-like cruelty which he knew was in Fargo, but more because of the uncertainty of the next few hours.

Fargo might be in town now as the words on the stable door had said. Whoever had written those words could be giving Fargo a hiding place within fifty yards of where Clint was standing. Perhaps he was watching from some attic window and laughing to himself as the contagion of panic spread through the town he hated.

Or suppose he came after dark? Where would he strike first? How many would be with him? And who was it in San Lorenzo who was helping him? That question more than any of the others bothered Clint because it was the key to where Fargo would go and what he would do and the kind of help he would receive.

Doc Julian? Sam Calloway? Doug Carney? All three had been in the stable. Any of them could have written that note on the back door. He shook his head and turned into the bank. It was simply incredible that one of the three would be involved with a man like Ben Fargo. Calloway and Carney had even been on the jury, and Doc Julian was a much loved doctor who had never to Clint's knowledge turned down an appeal for help.

Clint nodded at Mack Ferguson, the teller. "I want to see Doug."

Ferguson motioned to Carney's office. "He's alone. Go on back."

As he pushed the swinging gate open, the thought struck Clint that Doc Julian had come here as a young man just out of medical school. He had repeatedly asked for donations to build a hospital. Now, after all these years and constant appeals and numerous projects on the part of the Ladies' Aid, there was less than a thousand dollars in the hospital account.

Clint had heard him say he was owed over eight thousand dollars which he was unable to collect. He often took a chicken or a sack of potatoes or even a pig or steer for payment of a bill, and remarked ruefully that Judge Wallace was almost as hard to collect from as some of the poverty-stricken ranchers who eked out a living in the dry country south of town. Was it possible, Clint asked himself, that because of this kind of treatment, the medico had gone whacky enough to turn against the town and side with a man like Ben Fargo?

The door of Carney's office was open and Clint went in without knocking. "Thought I'd see how you were holding up, Doug."

Carney had been going through a pile of legal papers. Now he sat back, smiling gently. "Pretty well." He drew the pearl-handled .32 from his coat pocket and laid it on the desk in front of him. "I'm armed to the teeth, Clint. If Fargo shows up here, I'll shoot him between the eyes." Then he shook his head, the smile leaving his lips. "I don't know who I'm fooling."

"Well, nothing's happened yet. There's something I aimed to ask you this morning and I forgot it. Who is Cousin Phil?"

"Cousin Phil?" Carney's face was blank. "Why do you ask?"

"Ludlow checked on the last telegrams that went over the wire between here and Grand Junction. One of them was to you from Cousin Phil."

"Oh, that. I've been so worried about Fargo that I forgot all about Phil. I expect him this afternoon. He's my father's brother's son. He sold a ranch on the Arkansas below Pueblo and wants to buy around here. I told him the bank had some good property and I'd be glad to show it to him. Of course I didn't know Fargo was going to kick up this mess. I'm afraid Phil will wish he'd stayed on the Arkansas." Carney leaned forward, looking a little less like a diminutive Santa Claus than usual. "Why did you ask? I mean, it's nobody's business if my cousin comes to see me."

"No, of course not. It's just that I'd been in your home enough that I thought I'd heard of all your relatives."

Carney sat back, his hands folded over his ball of a belly, suddenly genial again. "Well, I'll tell you, Clint. Even after you're married, I expect you'll hear about relatives that you never knew existed."

"I suppose." Clint rose, and then said, "When you were in the livery stable this morning, did you notice anything out of the way?"

"No." Carney again leaned forward, an expression of anxiety on his round face. "I went in to see Shorty about a horse he has for sale, but he was gone. What was there to see?"

"Another message about Fargo. On the back door this time. It said he's here. I asked because I'd like to know when it was written."

Carney's face turned pale. He placed trembling hands on the desk as he whispered, "The hell! You think somebody's hiding him?"

"If he's in town. You didn't see the writing?"

"No, I sure didn't. I wasn't there very long. You know how it is in the back of the stable with the door closed. It's pretty dark."

"That's why Shorty didn't see it before. He doesn't know who wrote it or when it was written. Well, you'd better get home early, Doug. You'll be safer there than here in the bank."

Sweat dribbled down Carney's cheeks and from the tip of his chin. "I'll do that." He took a handkerchief from his pocket and wiped his face. "You drop around, Clint. Just to check up."

"I aim to," Clint said.

As he left the banker's office, he saw that Ferguson was

standing in the front door staring into the street. He turned when he heard Clint. "Ludlow. Brought a dead man in and then fell out of his saddle like he was dead himself."

Ludlow! Clint had never expected to see him again. He shoved past Ferguson and ran to where Ludlow lay in the dust. Sam Calloway and Pete Larson were with Doc Julian, who was bending over the sheriff. Julian rose when Clint got there.

"He brought Matt Smith in," the doctor said. "He was conscious for a minute or two. He said he found Matt dead, then somebody cracked him over the head and he didn't remember anything until he woke up in Matt's storeroom. Says he fainted a couple of times coming in. That's why he's so late."

Clint looked down at the unconscious man. So Fargo had got to Matt Smith ahead of Ludlow. He was ashamed of his cynical thought that Ludlow was not hurt as much as he was pretending.

"Pete, help Doc carry Matt inside," Clint said. "Sam, give me a hand with Tom. We'll get him to bed in his house."

"Two dead men," Doc Julian said, "One prisoner in jail. One sheriff knocked out and it's only half-past three. I'll come over and have a look at him, but I don't think he's going to be much help to you, Clint. He got a hell of a wallop."

"No, he won't be," Clint said. It didn't make much difference. He hadn't expected any.

FIFTEEN

DUKE WADE RODE INTO SAN LORENZO SHORTLY BEFORE four. He had intended to reach town sooner, but he had seen Ludlow riding slowly ahead of him. Not wanting to catch up with the sheriff or pass him, Wade had slowed down. He wasn't afraid that he'd be recognized; he simply didn't want to attract any more attention than was necessary.

The arrival of the sheriff with the body of a murdered man would create a stir, and if Wade arrived at approximately the same time, he'd naturally be involved in it. So, by holding back, he reached town a few minutes after Ludlow did.

Wade saw with satisfaction that Main Street was completely deserted. He grinned, thinking that this was like the day of a funeral. That's just about what it was, the funeral of the town of San Lorenzo. Fargo had said the town was afraid of him, and judging by appearances he was right.

Turning into the livery stable, Wade dismounted and slapped dust from his clothes. A small, oldish man came out of the back. He would be Shorty Bogardus, Wade thought, one of the jurymen Fargo aimed to kill. Crazy, Wade told himself. Completely crazy. He couldn't imagine a more harmless man than this dried-out little peanut who had voted with the other eleven the way he was supposed to.

Wade remembered Nan Carney and the Tebo boy. He'd talked Fargo out of killing them. Or had he? Sure, Fargo had agreed to play it Wade's way, but whether he meant to keep his promise was something else. Well, that situation would be met when the time came. If he had to pull the string on Fargo, he'd do it.

"I'm Doug Carney's cousin Phil," Wade said, holding his hand out to Bogardus. "I'll probably be here several days."

"I'm Shorty Bogardus." He nodded at the horse. "Looks like he's come a ways."

"He has," Wade said. "I sold my ranch on the Arkansas and thought I'd come over here and look around. Doug claims it's good country."

"It is," Bogardus said. "It surely is, but I don't mind telling you that you hit it at the wrong time."

"Must be an epidemic," Wade said. "I noticed there wasn't nobody on the street."

"It is, kind of," Bogardus agreed. "An epidemic of fear. It's contagious as hell. Ever hear of Ben Fargo?"

Wade shook his head. "No."

"Well, he was tried here in San Lorenzo and sent up for killing a calf. A mean son of a bitch if there ever was one. The rumor is that he broke out of the pen and he's coming to get square with us for sending him to Canon City. Was I you, mister, I'd stay at the hotel tonight."

"Why?"

"Doug Carney was foreman of the jury that convicted

Fargo. He'll come after Doug sure, so if you're in the house, you may get caught in some shooting."

Wade patted the gun at his side. "If Fargo comes nosing around, he'll be the one who gets caught in some shooting." He turned toward the archway, then swung back. "Bogardus, you said it was a rumor about Fargo coming?"

"That's what started it, but it's more'n that now. This morning the deputy, Clint Harper's his name, rode out to warn a fellow named Bill Ivor who was a juryman. Harper got into a fight with a couple of hardcases. He killed one and jailed the other one. Then just a few minutes ago the sheriff, Tom Ludlow's his name, rode in with the body of Matt Smith. Fargo had killed him. You see, Smith had been a juryman. So it's more'n a rumor when you've got two dead men."

"Sounds like it. Well, I'll go see Cousin Doug. I may be doing some riding tomorrow, so rub my horse down and give him a double bait of oats."

"I'll take care of him," Shorty promised. "Don't you worry none."

Wade walked rapidly to the bank, knowing he had called the time a little too close. Carney closed the front door at four, and that was only a few minutes away. As he hurried along the street, he reflected that it was only natural for Ludlow to think that Fargo had killed Matt Smith. That part was good, for it added to the fear that the townspeople had of Fargo. But the business of Harper shooting one of the men at the toll bridge wasn't good.

Wade had wanted to quiz Bogardus, but he'd been afraid of making him suspicious. If Muley Hanks was the one who had been shot, it would wreck part of the plan. It would wreck it if Hanks was in jail as far as that went. He was supposed to have fresh horses at the toll bridge. Now Wade and Fargo would have to get them here in town, probably from Bogardus' corral.

Wade had no idea who the man with Muley was. When

Wade had talked to him, he'd said he'd do the job himself, but he must have got worried at the last minute. Maybe he'd run into one of the old bunch and asked him to help out. Whoever it was, Wade and Fargo would have to break him out of jail before they left town. It wouldn't be hard, once Clint Harper was removed, but it would be an additional chore and would take time.

Wade reached the bank just as Mack Ferguson was drawing the shades at the front windows. Wade said, "I'm Doug Carney's cousin. I'd like to see him if he's in."

The teller was jumpy, but that was natural enough, Wade thought. He looked Wade over from his pale blue eyes and great beak of a nose on down his tall body. Then he said, "He's back in his office, but he didn't say anything about having a cousin."

"Probably forgot to mention me," Wade said. "I hear you're having some excitement."

"We sure are," Ferguson said, and motioned toward the closed door in the back.

Wade nodded amiably and pushed through the swinging gate beside the teller's cage. He walked on to the door of Carney's office and knocked. Carney opened the door, and when he saw who it was, he said heartily, "Phil, it's been a long time. Just get in?"

"A few minutes ago," Wade said. "I left my horse in the livery stable. The fellow there said the town was in trouble."

"I'm afraid so," Carney said. "Two killings already."

Wade stepped inside and Carney closed the door behind him. He said in a low tone, "That will convince Ferguson. If you go right to my place from here, I doubt that you'll meet anyone else."

"I didn't think anybody was left in town when I rode in," Wade said as he sat down in front of Carney's desk.

"It worked, all right," Carney said. "I wrote just three words on the livery stable door during the night. FARGO

IS COMING. That was all. Well, you should have been here. Just about everybody in town acted like a chicken with a hawk overhead. They headed for cover. Ludlow and Harper ran around warning everybody who had been on the jury, then they left town to tell Bill Ivor and Matt Smith. I was lucky enough to get into the stable when Bogardus was gone and write FARGO IS HERE on the back door. They didn't find it till this afternoon. Now most people think Fargo is hiding somewhere in town getting ready to cut loose."

"I noticed a lot of the blinds were down."

Carney nodded. "I never saw anything like it. Sam Calloway's still in his store. Bogardus is in the stable. Pete Larson kept the Gay Lady open, but he's about ready to run. Doc Julian's been in and out of his office. Clint Harper shows up on the street. Besides Ferguson and me, that's about it. Some of the others have left town and there'll be more by night. Fargo won't have to worry about anybody getting in his way. He can pick his men off any time he wants to."

Wade rolled and lighted a cigarette. There were usually good reasons for a man going bad and he thought he knew all of them. But this pot-bellied man who was respected in his community and had a good job just didn't fit any of the patterns. He hadn't understood Carney when they had first met in Montrose to set things up. He still didn't.

"Fargo bust out all right?" Carney asked.

"Slick as goose grease," Wade said. "All you need is enough money to make a good payoff." He jerked his head in the direction of the livery stable. "I had a talk with Bogardus. He said Harper shot a man."

Carney nodded. "Muley Hanks. Harper brought Happy Reese in."

"Reese?" Wade sat up, eyes questioning. "What'n hell was that drunk doing with Muley?"

"I don't know. I don't think it makes much difference. Reese couldn't have known about me."

"No, I guess he couldn't." Wade leaned back in his chair again, the cigarette dangling from one corner of his mouth. "I didn't tell Muley. No point to it. He wasn't real smart. Hiring Reese proves it." He scowled thoughtfully. "There's only two men in town who know me. One's Bill Ivor and the other one's Happy Reese. Oh yes, there's Doc Julian."

"Ivor will stay at the toll bridge and Reese will stay in jail. Doc won't be on the street much. He's got a baby coming any time now. You've got nothing to worry about as far as being recognized is concerned."

Carney scratched a cheek thoughtfully. "In fact, none of us have anything to worry about except Clint Harper. I hate to say this because it's going to be hard on Nan—she figures to marry him, you know—but he's dangerous. One of you will have to kill him first thing."

"Can't you take care of it?"

"I can but I won't because of Nan." Carney laid his pearl-handled .32 on the desk. "I'm going to kill just one man, Wade. The rest are up to you and Fargo. This morning Harper was talking to Nan about a Judas being in town. That's who I am, Wade, and this is the Judas gun. I'm going to kill Judge Wallace with it."

Wade was startled, but he did not let his face show his feelings. He and Fargo needed Carney for a few hours. After that he didn't care what happened to the banker. He doubted that Carney would live to see the sun come up in the morning, but that was apparently a thought which had never occurred to Carney. He went on the assumption that you could trust Ben Fargo to keep a bargain, an assumption that had cost a good many men their lives.

"I don't savvy how this deal started," Wade said. "How did Fargo know you'd play our game?"

"I contacted him," Carney said. "I've had this in my

mind for a long time. I saw him a few weeks before I talked to you. I told the warden I had a plan for Fargo when he got out, a decent job and all, but when I got to Fargo, I told him what I'd do in exchange for his promise he wouldn't hurt me and for half the money that's in the safe. He said he'd fix it so you'd get in touch with me."

"Why did you start it?" Wade asked curiously. "You've got nothing to gain."

"I have a hell of a lot to gain. In the first place, I wanted to be able to live without worrying about what would happen to me when Fargo got out. I was foreman of the jury, so he was bound to come after me. I bought a chance to rob Wallace's bank and lay it on somebody else. And I bought a chance to shoot Wallace and have it blamed on Fargo. It shouldn't make any difference to him how much he's blamed for now."

"No," Wade agreed. "It don't make no difference to me why you want to kill Wallace, but I'm curious."

Carney leaned forward, his face dark with the pent-up hatred that had festered in him for years. "Wade, you've never lived the way I have, knowing you were a nothing. You've always been important. Men have looked up to you. They've followed you. That right?"

"I guess so," Wade said vaguely. "I never thought much about it."

"I have," Carney said with a viciousness that surprised Wade. "I've been a nothing from the day I started working in this bank and that's been a long time. When you've had your butt kicked until it's so sore you can't sit down and your nose rubbed in horse manure time after time, and you know it'll never be any different as long as the son of a bitch is alive, then you begin to think of murder. Before I kill him, he'll know why I'm doing it. I'll tell him. Then I'll be something, in my own mind at least."

"Anybody else know how you feel?"

"Nobody. Not even Nan."

"You'll be dead tomorrow," Wade said. "Somebody's bound to find out you killed Wallace. For one thing, folks will wonder why your Cousin Phil left town so quick."

Carney shook his head. "Nobody will know except Nan, and she won't talk. As for you, I'll just say you got scared by what was happening and left before you got hurt. Maybe I'll take the money and leave, too. Or maybe I'll stay here and hide it if Wallace's widow wants me to run the bank. I'll see."

Wade rose, restless and vaguely uneasy at the way Carney explained his actions. Wade had no use for a Judas no matter which side he was on. He asked, "How will I get to your house?"

Carney gave him directions, then added, "Nan will be home soon. Be careful with her."

"I will," Wade promised, thinking that Carney had no idea what Fargo planned to do, of his way at hitting at Clint Harper by injuring Nan.

"Ferguson will leave in about an hour," Carney said. "After that I'll empty the safe and bring the money home in a leather case which I have often carried between the bank and the house. Nobody will suspect anything. I'll divide as soon as Fargo shows up, then both of you will have to get out."

Wade nodded again. "Fargo will be here about dark."

"Good." Carney held out his hand. "It should work out very well."

"Yes, I think it will," Wade said, and shook the banker's soft hand.

Carney replaced the gun in his pocket. "I'll see you about six."

Wade left the office. Ferguson got down from his tall stool by the window and let Wade out through the front door. Clint Harper was standing across the street, the only man in view. At least Wade guessed it was Harper, for he was a big man wearing a star.

As Harper crossed to him and he had a closer look, Wade thought he understood why Carney had said he must be killed first. Wade's impressions of people were usually right, and as he met Harper's gray eyes, he wondered how he'd make out if he drew against the deputy. Here was a man who wouldn't run, probably the only man in town who wouldn't.

"I'm the deputy sheriff, Clint Harper." He held out his hand. "This is a bad day for strangers to be in town. I thought you'd better be warned."

"I'm Phil Carney," Wade said as he shook hands. "Doug's cousin."

"Doug told me you were coming," Harper said pleasantly. "Did he tell you what was going on?"

"He sure did," Wade said. "I'm going to his house and stay inside. I'll leave it to you to take care of this fellow Fargo. Looks to me like he's got the town treed."

"I'm afraid he has," Harper agreed. "I'll be obliged if you will stay inside."

"Glad to have met you," Wade said, and turning, walked away.

There was a man, Wade thought, and realized with regret that they would be trying to kill each other in a few hours. It was a hell of a note, but it wouldn't be any other way. Then he wondered what Nan Carney looked like, and what he would have to do to save her life.

SIXTEEN

FROM A REAR WINDOW OF HER KITCHEN MARGE RAINER watched Clint and Sam Calloway bring Ludlow to his house. They came by way of the alley and across the back of the lot, Clint and Calloway holding him in the saddle. Ludlow was swaying from side to side like a straw man, his head tipped forward so that his chin rested on his chest.

Marge cried out involuntarily, a sound that brought Bonita running. "What is it, Marge ?"

"Look." Marge pointed at the three men. "I've got to go over there. He looks like he's almost dead."

"No." Bonita grabbed her arm. "If he was that bad off, Doc would have kept him in his office. You can't do anything for him."

"Oh, but I can. I'm a good nurse."

Bonita did not relinquish her grip on Marge's arm. "You can't go. This morning you said you guessed everyone knew about you and Ludlow, but you hadn't thought they did. If you go over there now and Sam Calloway sees you, everybody will know. You might just as well advertise it in the paper.''

Marge shook off Bonita's grip. She was remembering, all right, but now all the strong words she had planned to say to Tom Ludlow were forgotten. He was hurt and he needed her, and nothing else seemed important. It didn't matter whether she lost what was left of her reputation or not.

She started toward the door and stopped when Bonita said sharply, ''Marge, do you have to be as big a fool as I was over Ben Fargo?''

Marge stopped and wiped her face with her handkerchief. Her heart was pounding in her breast until she could hardly breathe. It would be embarrassing to go over there as long as Sam Calloway was in the house. She said heavily, ''All right, Bonita. I'll wait for a while. But I've got to know how badly he's hurt.''

Marge sat down beside the window so she could watch Ludlow's house. Bonita had been here most of the afternoon and now she was close to the breaking point. She had not gone back to the Wallace house and asked the Judge to send to the Box W for help as Clint had wanted her to. The girl simply hadn't been able to bring herself to do it.

''What am I going to do?'' Bonita had asked. ''I can't face the old devil again. I keep telling myself I've lived with him this long and I'd be crazy to lose all his money by walking out on him, but then I think he might live for months and I know that all the money in the world isn't worth it.''

''I'll go with you to see him if it will do any good,'' Marge had said.

''It wouldn't. He'd just raise hell.''

Now Marge leaned forward, watching Doc Julian, who had appeared in the alley. Crossing Ludlow's back yard, he went into his house. A moment later Sam Calloway left and turned toward the stable. Presently Shorty Bogardus appeared and took Ludlow's horse that had been standing a few feet from the back door. She would have to wait until Doc Julian left, Marge decided.

Bonita asked, "Is Calloway still there?"

"No, but Doc Julian is. Tom must be pretty bad off or Doc wouldn't be there so long."

"Maybe not," Bonita said. "Maybe Doc thinks he's safer with Clint than if he was in his office or on the street."

Marge turned to look at the girl. "What are you going to do if Clint comes over here and finds out you haven't gone back home?"

"Nothing, unless he tries to make me go," the girl said sullenly. "From now on nobody is going to make me do anything. If Clint tries it, I'll scratch his eyes out. I'll spit in his face."

Marge turned back to the window again. Bonita would probably do exactly what she said. This was something Marge did not understand, for she had always been a compliant person who tried to satisfy people. But Bonita was cast in a different mold. She must have received her defiant streak from her mother. She certainly couldn't have inherited it from her father.

Bonita, too restless to remain still, went to the front of the house. Marge lost all track of time as she waited. Presently Doc Julian came out of the house and hurried toward his office. As soon as he disappeared, she slipped through her back door, ran to Ludlow's house, and went in without knocking as she had done many times in the past.

Ludlow was flat on his back in bed, a bandage wrapped around his head. His eyes were closed and she thought for a moment he wasn't conscious, as pale as he was and completely motionless. Clint was standing on the other side of the room, a grim, gray-faced man who at this moment looked far older than he was.

"How is he?" she whispered.

"He's all right," Clint said with a biting contempt she did not understand. "It's a damned funny thing, Marge. You'd wonder who was sheriff, him or me."

She glared at him. He ought to have more sympathy for a man who had been seriously injured in the line of duty. She pulled up a chair and sat down beside the bed, her face to Ludlow who had opened his eyes and was looking at her.

"Hello, Marge," he said.

"Oh Tom." She took his hand and leaning down, kissed him on the cheek. "How do you feel?"

He groaned. "Like hell. I ran into Fargo in Matt Smith's house and he pistol-whipped me. He'd killed Matt. I brought his body in."

She felt like crying, for it seemed a miracle that Tom was still alive. She fought her emotions until she had them under control, then she looked back at Clint.

"What do you expect Tom to do? It's a wonder he isn't dead."

"It sure is," Clint said, "if he did run into Fargo."

She wasn't sure what he meant by that, but he didn't enlarge on it. He just stood scowling at her until he asked, "Have you seen Bonita?"

"She's in my house now."

"Did she go to the Judge and ask him to send to the Box W for help like I told her?"

"No. She couldn't, Clint."

"Why the hell couldn't she?"

"It wouldn't do any good. Nobody ever changes the Judge's mind. But it's more than that with her. She's waited on him hand and foot and he's treated her like a servant. She's just had all she can stand of it. I look for her to pack up her things and move out."

"The old man's helpless," he said. "Somebody's got to look out for him."

"Andy Downs can."

"Andy doesn't know he's supposed to."

"Well, I'll go up there and tell Andy after a while if she doesn't," Marge said.

"I'll tell her myself," Clint said angrily. "I don't care how she feels about the Judge. She married him and she owes him something."

He started toward the door. Marge said, "Clint." He turned, impatient with her. "You had some advice to give me this morning, Clint. Now I'll give you some. If you try to make Bonita do anything, you'll do nothing but stir up trouble. She said she'd scratch your eyes out and spit in your face. And she will. Now you'd better leave this to me. I'll see that it's done within an hour or so."

Clint stared at her, thoroughly angry, his lips squeezed together until they were white. "All right," he said, and went on out of the house. Crossing the back yard to the alley, he disappeared from her sight.

Marge turned to Ludlow. "Can I fix you something to eat? Or do anything to make you feel better?"

"Yeah, you can do something. Harper gone?"

"Yes."

"Then go to the livery stable and get me a fresh horse. I don't care if you buy or rent him. Just get me the fastest horse Bogardus has got."

This was the last thing she expected. She said, "You haven't got any business with a horse. You can't even stand. How do you think you can ride?"

He sat up on the side of the bed and jerked the bandage off his forehead. "I didn't fool Harper one damned bit. I can stand up and I can ride a horse. As soon as you get one for me, I'm riding out of here while I can."

She stared at him, thinking he was out of his mind. "I saw you riding in here while ago," she said. "Clint and

Sam Calloway were hanging onto you. You'd have fallen out of your saddle before you went fifty yards by yourself."

"Are you going to bring me that horse or not?"

He rose and stood facing her, impatient and angry. She put her hands on his arms. "What about us, Tom? You've said so many times we'd get married, but if you run out on Clint and the town this way, you'll never be able to come back."

"Sure, I'll marry you. Get two horses."

She stared at him for several seconds, knowing how completely right Clint had been. For the first time she saw Tom Ludlow stripped of his veneer of charm, without his glib talk and bright promises, a liar and a cheat and a coward.

She slapped him hard across the side of the face and whirled and ran out of the house. She heard him curse her and heard his pounding steps behind her and she thought he was coming after her. She lunged across her back porch and into the kitchen and slammed and locked the door, then looked through the window. He wasn't following. Instead, he had turned toward the livery stable.

Bonita ran into the kitchen. "What happened?"

Marge couldn't say anything. She pointed at Ludlow who was talking to Shorty Bogardus. They seemed to be arguing, then Bogardus went inside and in a few minutes returned with a saddled black gelding. Ludlow handed him some money and mounted and rode west out of town.

"Well," Bonita said smugly, "there goes your brave sheriff, Marge. You'll never see him again and I'd say you were better off."

Marge still couldn't say anything. She looked at the wall clock. Twenty minutes till five. Bonita was right, but it was hard to give up the last hope of a dream that had been so good, that had promised so much. She dropped into the chair beside the window, unable even to cry.

SEVENTEEN

NAN REMAINED AT SCHOOL UNTIL NEARLY FIVE TO FINISH grading papers and to look over the assignments for tomorrow. Ordinarily she would have taken her work home, but tonight she must not be tied down with anything after supper. She didn't want to be out after dark, either. She'd start the fire as soon as she got home, cook supper, and get a rig from Shorty Bogardus. She'd take Danny to the Hector place and be back while it was still light. She would do the dishes then.

She called to Danny, who was playing at the swings. He came running to her and they walked to the Carney house together, his hand in hers. He often came home with her to cut wood. He would stay for supper and sometimes even spend the night.

This was the way he liked to walk, Nan holding his hand, and she often puzzled over it. He was a cheerful ten-year-old, big for his age, with sandy hair, blue eyes, and a generous supply of freckles. In many ways he seemed old for his years, but in this matter of wanting her to hold his hand he was like a toddler who was seeking assurance of Nan's love.

When Nan had asked Danny's mother after school if she could keep him all night, Mrs. Tebo had been relieved. She'd said, "Of course he can stay." It seemed to Nan that after Dan Tebo's death a year ago, Danny's mother had resented the boy. Perhaps he found something in her, Nan thought, that was denied him by his mother.

Half a block from the Carney house, he looked up at Nan and grinned impishly. "Nan, you don't reckon Clint will come around tonight?"

She smiled. "You wouldn't want to see him, would you, Danny?"

"Sure I would. When are you getting married?"

"I don't know, Danny."

She tried to keep from thinking of what might happen tonight, but now she could not. The terrible fear gripped her that perhaps she would never marry Clint, that by morning he might be dead. She added, trying to keep her cheerful tone, "I expect it will be soon."

Danny glanced up at her, sensing that he had said something wrong, but not having any idea what it was. Both were silent until they reached Nan's back door, then she said, "You go on in and I'll fetch up some milk from the cellar."

He was sitting at the table when she came in with a crock of milk. She thought she smelled cigarette smoke, but decided she was imagining it, or that it came from someone who had gone by on the street. She poured a glass of milk for Danny, brought the cooky jar from the pantry, and gave him a handful.

Now the cigarette smell was stronger. Alarmed because she knew her father would not be home for another hour, she went into the front room. She stopped, her hand coming up to her throat.

A man was sitting in a rocking chair, his feet on a stool in front of him. He was smoking a cigarette, now and then flicking the ashes on the floor beside him. He was dirty, he hadn't shaved for some time, and it seemed to her he had the biggest, sharpest beak of a nose she had ever seen.

He rose when she came into the room and took off his hat. He said apologetically, "I hope you don't mind me smoking in the house, ma'am. Nobody was here when I came in, so I just rolled me one and fired up."

"Who are you?"

She leaned against the wall, not sure her knees would hold her. For a terrifying moment she had been afraid this man was Ben Fargo, waiting for her father to come home so he could kill him. But now she was sure he wasn't Fargo. His eyes were pale blue and Fargo's were brown. Fargo was a better-looking man. Even prison wouldn't produce the beaklike nose this fellow had.

He winked at her. "I'm surprised you don't know me, Nan. I'm your father's Cousin Phil. I sold my ranch on the Arkansas and I came here to look the country over. Doug said you could put me up while I look for a ranch."

For a moment she thought she had gone crazy. It seemed to her she must have stepped into some other life, or she had somehow become another person. She was sure of one thing. Her father, Douglas Carney, had never had a brother. There could not be a Cousin Phil.

"Wait here," she said.

She went into the kitchen where Danny was on his sixth cooky and second glass of milk. She said, "I'll need the rest of the cookies for supper. You'd better get started." As he got up, she patted him on the back. "Be sure you cut me a nice pile of kindling. I'll call you when supper's ready."

He got up, then stood motionless staring past Nan. She turned to see the stranger standing in the doorway looking curiously at the boy. She was angry because he hadn't stayed in the front room where she had told him to, but she was able to control her voice when she said, "Danny, this is Cousin Phil. He's here to look for a ranch."

"Howdy, Danny," the man said pleasantly.

Danny walked to him and held out his hand. "I'm pleased to meet you, Cousin Phil." The man shook hands with him, then Danny added, "You look more like a gunslinger than a cowboy."

"Why, I just carry a gun for rattlesnakes and such," the man said. "I'm a cowboy all right."

"Run along, Danny," Nan said.

He walked as far as the door, then stopped and said, "I'll bet you can't draw as fast as Clint Harper. He's the fastest there is."

"I sure don't want to draw against him if he's that fast," the man said, laughing.

Danny went outside. When the door closed, Nan turned to the range and built a fire, her hands trembling so that she was clumsy. The man said, "Let me do it."

"All right." She stepped back from the stove. "Now then. You can tell me who you are. I don't want to hear any more about Cousin Phil."

"Who's the kid?" he asked.

"Danny Tebo."

He swore and whirled to face her. "What's he doing here?"

"He often comes home with me and cuts wood. Dad doesn't like to do the chores and Danny needs a little pocket money."

The man turned back to the range, and when he had the fire going, he said, "You might just as well have both barrels. You'll find out when your pa gets home anyway. I'm Duke Wade. You've heard of me?"

She nodded, too shocked to say anything. He went on, "Ben Fargo will be here after while. Your pa is going to clean out the safe and fetch the money home with him.

We'll divide, then me'n Ben will get out. We have some chores to do, and when they're done, we'll ride out of town and stay out."

She backed up until she came to a chair. She sat down as the room began to whirl in front of her. She was overcome by a night-marish feeling of unreality. This couldn't be happening; what he'd said couldn't be the truth.

"You're . . . you're lying," she finally managed to say.

He shrugged. "You can think what you want to," Wade said, "but your pa will be home about six with a satchel of money. I guess you'll know then I ain't lying."

He wasn't lying. She was as sure of that as she could be sure of anything in the half-conscious state she was in. "Why?" she whispered. "Why would Dad do a thing like that?"

"You'll have to ask him. All I can tell you is that he's helping us. In return, Ben promised he wouldn't kill him, even though he was foreman of the jury that sent Ben to prison. Besides, it seems your pa has been wanting to get old Judge Wallace. This way he blames the robbery on me'n Ben, and he can hide his part of the money till it blows over and nobody will suspect him."

She believed Wade now. She couldn't help it, for she knew how worried her father had been about what Fargo would do to him when and if he got out of prison. She knew, too, how much her father hated Judge Wallace, how the old man had belittled him in every way he could over the years, even on a thing like foreclosing on Clint's ranch. Wallace had repeatedly told Clint and everyone else that he left bank business to Doug Carney, whereas the truth was, according to her father, that Wallace made every decision and then publicly blamed him for the unpopular ones.

"What am I supposed to do?" she asked finally.

"You and the kid will stay here," he said. "I'm sorry about that, but I can't take any chances on your going to

Harper or sending a message with the kid. You'll cook supper for me along with the rest of your family. Be sure you've got something for Ben to eat when he gets here. I don't reckon you'll make us any trouble after we leave, with your pa in the deal up to his neck. If you do, we'll come back and shoot both of you, and that's something I wouldn't want to do."

Wade paused, chewing on his lower lip a moment, then added, "Ben would, though. He's worse'n he used to be. Prison's changed him for the worst, so when he gets here, go easy. Whatever you do, don't make him mad."

For a long moment she sat motionless, thinking of all the things she had heard about Duke Wade: killer, horse thief, cattle rustler, bank robber. Yet she did not sense in him the evil, the inherent meanness, which she had felt in Ben Fargo all through the trial.

"All right," she said. "Get out of the kitchen so I can start supper."

"Sure." He grinned at her in his easy way. "There's another thing I'd better tell you. Ben swears he'll kill two men before he leaves town. One's the Judge, the other one's your friend Clint Harper. There's really three, counting Tom Ludlow, but I've got a hunch he ain't hanging around town to give Ben a chance at him. Ben's got some notions about the other jurymen like Bogardus and Calloway, but maybe I can talk him out of that. We just ain't got the time."

He left then. She hurried with the potatoes and meat, and started warming a pot of beans that had been left from last night. All the time she was searching her mind for some way to warn Clint. She could not think of anything. She didn't even know what she would do if he dropped in as he often did after supper—and as he had said he would tonight. He would be killed, and then Fargo would turn on them and kill them. Danny Tebo, too.

She groaned as she considered the magnitude of the

mistake she had made. Danny would have been safer anywhere than he was here. She wouldn't be able to take him to the Hector place. Wade wouldn't let her leave the house. If she could think of some way to get Danny out of the house. . . .

Her father came in then. She heard him talk briefly to Wade and then go into his bedroom. She ran after him, but Wade caught her by an arm before she reached the door and shook her roughly.

"I've been watching you," he said. "You keep peeking out at the kid. Now get this straight. Get it God-damned straight. If that kid ain't here for supper and the rest of the evening, you and your pa are dead. Savvy?"

She tried to jerk free, but he held her so hard he bruised her arm. "I wouldn't want to do it, but I will if I have to. Ben and me planned this too long to miss now. Your pa did the writing on the stable and it worked like we figured. The town's scared. By dark it'll just about be empty and that's the way we want it. This is our chance to make a big haul. We'll get across the state line and head for Mexico. That's why the kid's got to be here. If he ran off and told Harper, he'd raise hell with us."

She nodded, too frightened to speak. He let her go and she ran into her father's bedroom. The only gun in the house was the pearl-handled .32 her father had carried to the bank that morning. If she could get that gun from him, she'd kill Wade. She knew she could. She'd have no more regret than if she'd killed a rattlesnake. Then she and Danny would get out of the house and find Clint. At the moment she didn't care what happened to her father. He had brought this down on himself.

But when she had entered his room and saw the pile of currency he had dumped on the bed, she realized she could never persuade him to give her the gun. She could only stand there with her back to the door and ask, "Why, Dad? Why?"

He glanced at her, smiling, his pink-cheeked face as innocent as Danny Tebo's freckled one. "Wade told you?" She nodded, and he said, "I'm sorry I couldn't tell you before, but it's not a thing I could make you understand. There were two reasons, Nan. First of all I bought safety for you and me. Sooner or later Fargo would get out, and I knew that unless I went to him and offered to be his friend, he'd kill me and probably you, too, simply because you were my daughter. The other reason is something I hope you will understand. It's important to me. You know how I've worked for Wallace all these years for a pittance, a mere pittance, and taken all of his . . ."

He stopped and straightening up, sucked in his belly. "Nan, this is a question of being nothing or something. It's simple when you see it that way. Now go finish supper."

She obeyed, struggling to hold back her tears. She couldn't break down now. She could tell herself that her father had gone crazy, and she could understand why he had lost his mind and gone into a crooked deal like this. She knew what Wallace had done to him just as she knew what the old man had done to Bonita and to Clint and many others.

Maybe it hadn't been so bad with the rest. Not for as many years anyway. Now, with the wisdom of hindsight, she realized she should have seen this coming. Her father had dropped little hints now and then that it wasn't always going to be this way.

She shouted for Danny to come to supper, then called her father and Wade. As they ate, Danny chattered away as uninhibited as ever, and Wade, amiable enough, answered his questions. After they finished eating, Danny challenged Wade to a game of checkers and Wade accepted. They played in the front room while Nan did the dishes.

The sun was down by the time she had finished, and

twilight was bringing lamps to life in the houses along the street. Fargo would be here soon, she thought. She still didn't know what she'd do when he arrived. It was not until she went into the front room to light the lamp for Danny and Wade that she realized her father was gone.

EIGHTEEN

CLINT WORE OUT THE TAG END OF THE AFTERNOON WALKING around town. Every minute seemed to drag. He was reasonably sure that Fargo was not in town, but there was a small chance the man was hiding in someone's house. If he saw Clint on the street, he might come into the open. Clint knew he was making a target of himself, but anything was better than this nerve-shattering suspense which might go on for hours.

If anything, the town grew more quiet as the hours passed. Finally, driven by restlessness he could not control, Clint saddled his horse and took a wide swing east of town, thinking that if Fargo planned to reach town about dusk he might catch the outlaw riding in. But he saw no one. He returned to the stable and put his horse up just as Mom and Lafe Risdon left town in their buggy.

''The town about empty?'' Clint asked Shorty Bogardus as he watered his horse behind the stable.

''Damned near it,'' Shorty said in disgust. ''Pete Larson

locked up the Gay Lady and left with his woman a while ago. A man can't even buy a drink in town now" Shorty glanced at Marge's house just as she came out of the back door and walked toward them. He added in a low tone, "Tom Ludlow got over his headache. He got a horse and pulled out."

"I'm not surprised," Clint said.

"But he's the sheriff," Shorty burst out. "It's his responsibility, not yours."

"It's not so much a question of whose responsibility it is, Shorty," Clint said, "as it is of who's going to accept it. I guess it's a good thing Tom left. Long as he was here he was the boss, and it's hell to take orders from a man you don't trust."

"Yeah," Shorty conceded, "I guess it is."

Marge came up to them, pale and tight-lipped. Clint saw that she had been crying. He said, "Well, nothing's happened yet."

She shook her head. "You're wrong, Clint. A lot has happened." She ran the tip of her tongue over dry lips. "If you haven't had supper, will you come over and eat with me?"

"Glad to," Clint said. "I'd clean forgot about it being supper-time."

"There's enough for you, Shorty," Marge said, "if you want to come."

"Thank you kindly," Shorty said, "but I'd better stay here. I'll be out front, Clint. If I see that murdering son, I'll come a-running."

"You do that," Clint said.

He walked back to Marge's house beside her, sensing her desperate need for company. He wondered what she would do with Ludlow gone. Clint doubted that the man would ever come back, now that he had given way to fear. But Marge said nothing until Clint had washed and she had placed the food on the table.

"Well, say it," she said. "Tell me you were right and I was a fool to believe anything Tom ever said to me."

"I don't operate that way, Marge," he said sharply. "You ought to know that."

"I do. I'm sorry. I guess I'd feel better if I could get mad at you and have a quarrel. Anyhow, you were right and I was a fool. After you left this afternoon, Tom got up and wanted me to bring him a horse. I wouldn't do it, so he went to the stable and got one and rode out of town."

Marge had filled her plate, but now she found she couldn't eat. She sat staring at the food until he finished. He said, "Mom Risdon locked up and left town. If you hadn't fed me, I'd have gone hungry."

She acted as if she didn't hear him. She said, "Bonita left quite a while ago. She was going to get a few things and tell the Judge she wouldn't spend the night there. She said she'd come right back, but she hasn't."

"I'll go up there and take a look," Clint said.

He rolled and lighted a cigarette, suddenly aware that the sun was down and the light here in Marge's kitchen was very thin. He had not realized it was so late. He said, "Thanks for the supper, Marge. I've got to get moving. Fireworks may start any time."

"Clint, you're alone, aren't you?"

"Looks that way," he answered. "I'll stop and see Sam Calloway on my way to the Judge's house. I'll get him to stay on Main Street while I scout around. Once it's dark, we've got no way of knowing when or where Fargo will hit."

"Let me help you, Clint," she said. "I can shoot. You've got a lot to live for. I haven't."

He went to her and put an arm around her. "You stay here. I may need you before morning and I'll want to know where I can find you. I don't want to hear any more talk about you not having anything to live for. You'll get over this."

"I suppose I will," she said tonelessly. "I was so happy when we were on the ranch. Now I guess it's only right that I make up for it. What is it the Bible says about rain falling on the just and the unjust?"

"It's something like that," he said, and left the house.

He saw Doc Julian hurrying toward the Delong place, his black bag in his hand. It was Mrs. Delong's time, Clint thought. He considered that for a moment, thinking it strange that a new life should be started on this night when others would certainly be ended. No, it wasn't strange at all; it was the way nature . . .

As he approached Sam Calloway's house, Clint suddenly stopped, flat-footed, unable to believe what he saw. Even in the thin dusk light he could not be mistaken. Sam Calloway had hitched up his hack and it stood in front of his house. The kids were climbing in, and Mrs. Calloway was seated in front.

Clint ran toward the hack, seized by a quick and violent anger. The one man he had counted on was running out on him. He reached the vehicle just as Calloway came out of the house carrying a Winchester.

"You can't go, Sam," Clint said. "I need you."

"Come on, Sam," Mrs. Calloway ordered. "Harper, you let him be. I don't want to be left a widow with all these kids. Mom Risdon told me Fargo was coming with fifty outlaws and they are going to put a torch to the town and kill everybody in it. If you had any sense, Clint Harper, you'd leave, too."

He whirled to face her. "Yeah, if I had any sense, I'd . . ."

She had a shotgun in the seat beside her. Now she picked it up and lined it on Clint. "You just shut your mouth and leave Sam be. You hear me?"

Clint stepped aside. "All right, Sam." He took a long breath, fighting his temper. If this was Sam Calloway's caliber, he didn't want his help any more than he wanted

Tom Ludlow's. He said, "I thought you were a man, Sam, but I was sure wrong. I wonder who's the father of these kids?"

Calloway didn't try to defend himself. He couldn't even look at Clint as he stepped up beside his wife and took the lines from her and spoke to the team. Mrs. Calloway was screaming obscene words at Clint, and did not stop until Sam slapped her across the face.

For a moment Clint stood watching as the hack rolled westward out of town. He thought, If I live, what will they say to me tomorrow when they come back, Sam and Pete Larson and the rest of them?

He started up the slope toward the Wallace house, knowing what they would say. He was a lawman, wasn't he? It was his job to stay and fight and maybe get killed, wasn't it? It was what he was paid for, wasn't it?

They might be honest in saying those things. For some of them, Pete Larson and Lafe Risdon and others, there would be no problem. Nothing had been expected from them; they were the leaners. But it would be different with Sam Calloway. He would never be able to look Clint in the face again. He would likely sell out and leave San Lorenzo and take his shame with him.

Clint was halfway up the hill when he saw Bonita top the crest above him and run toward him, her skirt flying. She stumbled and fell, but by the time he reached her she was on her feet again. She would have gone on past him without seeing him if he hadn't caught her and held her. She was crying hysterically and shaking as if she had a chill. He couldn't get her to tell him what had happened; he wasn't even sure she heard what he was asking.

With an arm around her, he led Bonita down the hill to Marge's house. Something terrible had happened up there in the big house, something so terrible that it had momentarily stunned her. And Clint could think of nothing worse than the appearance of Ben Fargo.

Bonita had calmed down by the time he got her into a chair in Marge's front room. Marge lighted a lamp, took a look at the girl's stricken face, and then glanced at Clint. "I don't know whether she's going to be able to say anything or not."

"Have you got any whisky?"

Marge nodded. "I'll get it."

Clint knelt in front of the girl, rubbing her hands and talking gently to her. He would have gone after Doc Julian if he hadn't known the doctor was with Mrs. Delong. All he could do was to hope that Bonita would come out of it. Marge returned with the whisky and gave Bonita a drink, placing an assuring arm around her shoulders.

Several minutes passed before her eyes lost their glassy expression. She began to cry, softly now, without the hysterical shaking that she had been unable to control. Marge gave her a handkerchief and she wiped her eyes.

"What happened?" Clint said. "I'm going up there, but I'd like to know what it was before I do. Did you see Fargo?"

"No, it wasn't Fargo," Bonita whispered. "It was Doug Carney. He killed the Judge. Then he ran into Andy Downs and was afraid Andy had seen what he'd done. He killed Andy." She swallowed, and then added with an effort, "Andy's lying on the porch in front of the door."

Clint sat on the floor in front of the girl, trying not to let his expression reveal his conviction that the girl was lying. She might have done the killing herself and then realized she must lay it on someone else. But Bonita had picked the wrong man when she named Doug Carney. He couldn't even cut off a chicken's head. He was that squeamish. When Clint hadn't been around to kill a rooster for Sunday dinner, Nan had done it herself.

Marge got another drink down Bonita. The girl shivered, and stared at the floor. She said, "I went up there and told the Judge I wasn't staying unless he sent for help.

We had a big row the way we always do when I try to get him to do something. He wouldn't listen to me. Said for me to go to hell. If I didn't want to stay in my home where I belonged, I could go and stay away. He'd change his will in the morning. He was hungry, so I fixed him something to eat, then he told me to get Andy Downs. They'd handle Fargo if he showed up.

"I went out to the carriage house where Andy has a room. I told him to come in and that I was leaving as soon as I packed some things. Andy was eating supper, but he said he'd come after he cleaned up his dishes."

She blew her nose and sat back, wadding up her handkerchief in her hand. "I went upstairs to my room and put what I'd need for the night in a bag. I heard somebody talking in the Judge's room and I thought it was Andy, although I hadn't heard him on the stairs. Then there was a shot. I couldn't move for a minute. I was scared because I thought it was Fargo. I heard someone running down the stairs and I opened the door a crack and saw Doug Carney. I guess he met Andy coming to the house. I heard two more shots. Carney kept on running."

"You didn't see his face?" Clint asked.

"No, but I saw his back. It was getting dusk, but there was enough light to see who it was. There isn't anyone in town I could mistake for Carney, is there? Nobody else built like him?"

Clint still didn't believe her, but he said, "No, I guess not."

"Well, I went into the Judge's room. He'd been shot in the chest. He was dead. I think I fainted. I was on the floor when I came to. I looked at the Judge again, and then I ran because I felt guilty. I guess I was afraid you'd think I killed him. In a way I was guilty. I wanted him dead and now he was. I saw Andy lying there in front of the door when I left the house. I don't remember anything after that."

Clint rose. He said to Marge, "She can't stay here. Fargo will look for her here when he doesn't find her in Wallace's house. Take her to the hotel. Maybe you'd better stay with her."

Marge shook her head. "No, I've got nothing to worry about. I'll come back here."

"All right," Clint said. "I'm going up there and take a look."

He strode rapidly up the slope again, still thinking about Bonita's fantastic accusation against Doug Carney. If she had named anyone but Doug! Well, there were two possible explanations. It could have been Fargo. Bonita, still in love with the man, might be trying to give him an alibi. Or it could have been Bonita herself, and she might have named the first man she had thought of.

He found Andy Downs's body on the porch just as Bonita had said. It was dark now, and he had to light a match to see where Downs had been shot. One bullet had grazed his neck, the other had caught him in the forehead just above the right eye.

Clint rose and went into the dark house. He thought bitterly that Andy was a man who had never harmed anyone, that he had died simply because he had been at the wrong place at exactly the wrong second of time.

He found a lamp, lighted it, and climbed the stairs to Wallace's room. The old man was dead, all right, shot in the chest and at close range. The bullet hole had been made by a small-caliber gun. Clint remembered that the hole in Downs's forehead had been about the same size.

All the time that Bonita had been talking, Clint had kept his mind closed to the possibility that she was telling the truth. Suddenly he remembered the little revolver Carney had shown him that morning. He remembered, too, that Pete Larson had said he'd seen Carney go into the stable, so he could have done the writing on the back door. Finally there was the mysterious Cousin Phil who wasn't Fargo, but could be one of Fargo's old bunch.

Then Doug Carney must be the Judas Clint had been seeking, and the little, pearl-handled .32 must be the Judas gun.

Clint whirled and ran recklessly down the stairs and out of the house, thinking that Nan might still be at home with Danny Tebo. Clint had been remiss in not watching the house closer than he had. Whether Fargo was there or not, Doug Carney was in trouble. But how could Clint arrest the father of the girl he was going to marry when that arrest would probably lead to the gallows?

NINETEEN

NAN CARNEY WAS IN THE FRONT ROOM WATCHING DANNY Tebo and Duke Wade play checkers when she heard the back door open. She supposed it was her father coming back. It had been fully dark for some time. She turned to ask him where he had been, but no words came. She froze, her mouth open, her eyes wide and staring.

It was Ben Fargo! She had known he would be here, probably soon after dark. Still, she had not been prepared for the sight of him. She had not seen him since that dramatic moment in the courtroom when he had screamed his threats at the Judge and jury and everyone else who had been responsible for what he had called, "A dirty job of railroading."

Then he had been freshly shaven, clean, and dressed in a store suit. He was none of those things now. He was filthy, he was wearing a ragged shirt and pants that didn't fit him and had probably been stolen from some clothesline between here and Canon City, and his face was covered with stubble.

He closed the back door and crossed the kitchen, glancing briefly at Nan and then fixing his eyes on Wade, who looked up and said casually, "I thought you'd be showing up pretty soon." He made a move and Danny jumped two of his men, and he said in disgust, "Oh hell."

The stench of Fargo's body pervaded the room. At the time of the trial he had been a big man, a little on the fleshy side, but now he was fried down to hide and bone, with a gauntness that gave his face an animal-like appearance.

At first Nan thought of a dog, then of a coyote. That was it, a coyote slipping into a barnyard to steal anything he could. But there was a difference. A coyote was never really dangerous. Ben Fargo was.

She stepped back to get farther away from the smell, her eyes fixed on his face as if she were hypnotized. She had no reason to think he would harm her. She had never injured him in any way. Still, she could not keep from trembling. A prickle ran along her spine like an electric charge. She was fascinated just as she would have been fascinated by a rattlesnake. She sensed that she had never seen a more completely dangerous man than Ben Fargo.

Danny had not looked up from the checkerboard, probably thinking it was Doug Carney who had come in, but he glanced up now, and grunted in surprise. Then, like Nan, he seemed fascinated and couldn't take his gaze from Fargo's face.

"Who's the kid?" Fargo asked Wade.

"Oh, just a neighbor kid who dropped in for supper," Wade said carelessly. "Talked me into a checker game and he's whipping me." The outlaw jerked his head at Nan. "Get him something to eat."

Fargo motioned for Nan to stay where she was. He said again, "Who's the kid?"

"I'm Danny Tebo," the boy said. "You're Ben Fargo, ain't you?"

"That's right, sonny," Fargo said.

"My father was Dan Tebo and he was on the jury that sent you to prison."

Nan thought the boy had more sense. She wanted to scream at him to shut up, that he was making a bad situation worse, but she couldn't say a word.

A wicked grin tugged at the corners of Fargo's mouth. "You're right again, sonny." He nodded at Nan. "Now you can get me something to eat." He brought his gaze back to the boy. "This is lucky finding you here, Tebo. Real lucky."

"You're letting him alone, Ben," Wade said. "You promised. Remember?"

"Yeah, I remember. Where's Carney?"

"I don't know. He slipped out after supper and I ain't seen him since, but it don't make any difference. He brought the money when he came home."

"Don't make any difference?" Fargo said angrily. "Why, you boneheaded fool, it makes all the difference. He might have gone after Harper."

Wade pushed his chair back. "You're the fool, Ben. You know better."

"All right, all right," Fargo said irritably. "Kid, you come into the kitchen where I can keep an eye on you."

Danny didn't argue. He rose and walked into the kitchen, Fargo following. He motioned for Danny to sit down at the table. The boy obeyed and Fargo took a chair across from him. Nan brought meat, potatoes, and beans, then poured his coffee. He ate ravenously and noisily, drank three cups of coffee, and bolted the slab of dried apple pie that Nan gave him.

Fargo sat back and belched, then rolled a cigarette as he said, "You're a good cook, ma'am." He struck a match and held the flame to his cigarette just as Doug Carney came in through the back door. The banker was visibly jolted when he saw Fargo. Nan, watching her father, knew how he felt. Just looking at Fargo was enough to shock anyone who had known him before he had gone to prison.

Carney recovered immediately and crossed the room to Fargo. He held out his hand. "I'm glad to see you, Ben. Nan find enough for you to eat?"

Fargo gave the banker's hand a quick shake and dropped it as if the feel of it was unpleasant. He said, "Wade says you fetched the money."

"I sure did," Carney said with false heartiness. "I'll get it."

Fargo rose, and motioned for Nan and Danny to go ahead of him. They obeyed, Nan taking the boy's hand and finding it clammy. Hers probably was, too, she thought.

She found it hard to realize this was really happening. She'd had nightmares that seemed to go on and on just as this one was doing. But it was no nightmare. Not even in her wildest dreams would she have conjured up anything as fantastic as what her father had done.

Why? She had been asking herself that ever since he had admitted to her that what Wade had said was true. Still she had no answer that made sense to her.

She stood by the table in the front room, holding Danny's left hand in her right, and looked at Fargo's thin face. The corners of his mouth were pulled down and his eyes were half closed. She turned away, trembling so violently that she wondered if the others heard her teeth chattering.

In that terrible, prescient moment she saw what lay ahead for them. It was as if death was already in the room. Even in the short time that Fargo had been in the house, his nerves had become tighter and tighter until he was like a charge of dynamite, capped and ready to explode. It would take only a slight jar to set him off.

Desperately she turned to Duke Wade who was watching

Fargo. Wade knew, too, she told herself, but she wasn't sure what the outlaw would do when the crucial moment came. Her father thought he had bought safety, but he had not, although she was sure he didn't know it yet. Whatever fate he met would be of his own doing, but she had done nothing to deserve death, and neither had Danny Tebo.

She took a step toward the door, then stopped, afraid that even such a small movement might be all it would take to set Fargo off. Their only chance was for Clint to come. He had said he would drop in to check up on them, but if he didn't come soon, it would be too late.

Then the thought struck her that Clint might walk in, not suspecting that Fargo was here, and that he might die before she could warn him. But she would warn him, somehow, and if she died because of it, at least she might be the means of saving Clint's life.

Carney walked out of the bedroom carrying a bulging flour sack. "Your plan worked well, Ben," Carney said, smiling ingratiatingly at Fargo. "The town's just about deserted. Even Ludlow left this afternoon. Harper's still here. So is Shorty Bogardus. And Doc Julian."

"What about Bonita?" Fargo demanded.

"I don't know," Carney said. "I guess she's in town somewhere, but she wasn't at home a few minutes ago." Carney set the flour sack on the table beside the checkerboard. "There's a little over fifteen thousand dollars here which is what I told you there would be. Most of it's in paper. A little gold. Do you want to look at it?"

"No," Fargo said. "Get the rest of it."

"The rest of it?" Carney looked as if he had been struck. "Ben, that's my share. Don't you remember our bargain?"

"The only bargain I ever make is for Ben Fargo. I said get it."

Doug Carney was not a brave man, but he had planned this for a long time and he could not bring himself to give up the money that was supposed to be his. He said, his voice high, "Ben, the rest of it is mine. I've taken chances, same as you and Wade. If anybody had seen me do that writing . . ."

"Get it," Fargo shouted. "God damn you, get it."

Carney fled into the bedroom. Wade said, "You made a bargain like he's claiming, Ben. You used to be a man who kept his word."

"Keep out of it, Duke," Fargo said. "I'm running the show."

Nan took another step toward the door, making a motion with her right hand. She wanted Danny to move with her so that when the blowup came, they'd have a chance to get out. She wasn't sure that Danny saw the slight movement of her hand, but Fargo let her know that he did. He seemed to be aware of everything.

"You ain't nothing to me either way, ma'am," Fargo said, "except that I aim to mark you up some for Harper to see before I kill him. The kid here does mean something. I don't care enough about Bogardus and Calloway to hunt 'em up. I'll kill 'em if I find 'em, but I ain't gonna waste a hell of a lot of time looking for 'em. But Harper's important. So's Wallace. I'll kill 'em both before I leave town. The money's important. So's Bonita. I'm telling you this so you'll know what I'm going to do and you can tell Harper after I'm ready to let you go. Now I'll tell you something. You make a run for the door and I'll shoot you."

"No you won't, Ben," Wade said. "You're forgetting what we agreed on."

"You keep sticking your nose into this, Duke," Fargo said, "and you'll get it, too. I've been thinking about what I'd do when I got back here ever since they took me to Canon City. I don't care how much riding we've done together or how much you've helped me. I'm having my fun tonight the way I want it. You'd just better stay out of it."

Carney returned with the satchel he had used to move the money from the bank to his home. He looked physically sick as he set the satchel beside the flour sack. He said bitterly, "This isn't right, Fargo. Not after you promised and what I've done for you. I killed the Judge tonight and saved you the trouble. All you've got to do now is to find Harper and then get out of town."

"You killed Wallace?" Fargo was visibly jolted for the first time since he had come into the house. "You're lying."

"Not much I am," Carney said with pride. "I killed him, all right. If you don't believe it, go up there to his fine house and see. He knew I was going to do it before I did and he knew why. You had just one thing to hate him for. I had a thousand. Every day I worked for him . . ."

Fargo yanked his gun from his waistband and lunged at Carney. He brought the barrel down across the top of Carney's head in a vicious blow that drove the banker to his knees. He struck again and again, all the time yelling like a madman, "I was going to kill him, you bastard. I'd been dreaming about it for two years and now you've kept me from it."

Nan ran for the door, screaming, "Run, Danny, run."

She heard Wade yell, "Ben! Stop it, Ben!"

She was through the door when she looked back. Wade drew his revolver, but he didn't get off a shot. Fargo had his gun in his hand. He whirled, firing as he turned. Wade was hit. She saw him start to fall. She didn't see anything else, for she was running and running, across the porch and the yard and on into the street. Fargo lunged to the door and fired two shots into the darkness after her.

Nan screamed, "Clint! Clint!" She was half a block from the house before she realized that Danny Tebo was not with her.

TWENTY

CLINT WAS MORE THAN A BLOCK FROM THE CARNEY house when he heard the first shot. He began to run, cursing himself for overlooking a possibility that now seemed obvious. He had promised to stop in just to check up. He should have done it sooner, but it hadn't occurred to him that Fargo would strike first at Doug Carney.

Clint had been certain Judge Wallace would be Fargo's first victim. But Carney had killed Wallace and Andy Downs, and that put a new face on the whole situation. Clint didn't know what the connection was between Carney and Ben Fargo, but there had to be one. Perhaps the gunfire didn't indicate that Fargo had struck at Carney, but Clint was willing to gamble that it did indicate that Fargo was in the Carney house.

Clint heard Nan scream his name; he heard two more shots and saw the ribbons of gunflame flash into the darkness from Carney's front porch. He called to Nan and then she was in his arms, sobbing hysterically. He held her hard for a moment and let her cry. Staring past her, he saw that the windows and the open door of the Carney house were bright with lamplight, but from where he stood here in the street, he couldn't see any movement inside the house.

Then he remembered Danny Tebo, and he shook Nan, demanding, "Did you take Danny out to the Hector place?"

She stopped crying, but continued to tremble. Her face was buried against his chest and it was a moment before she could answer.

"No," she said finally. "I couldn't."

He was furiously angry with her then because he had planned so carefully to get Danny out of danger and Nan had understood the situation. Now all that he had succeeded in doing was to drag Danny into greater danger than if he had left the boy home.

"Why?" He gripped Nan by the shoulders and shook her. "Why couldn't you?"

"Duke Wade was in the house when I got home. He wouldn't let either one of us leave."

"Duke Wade?" This hit Clint hard. He had been reasonably sure that Fargo would not be alone, but it had never occurred to him that he would have as his partner the notorious Duke Wade. But at the moment Wade wasn't important. Now that Nan was safe, Danny was the one to worry about. "Where is Danny?"

"I don't know. I ran when the shooting started. I thought he was with me. He could have gotten away, too."

"Then Fargo's got him?"

"I guess so. But he may have killed him by now."

Clint pushed her aside and ran toward the Carney house. "Clint," Nan cried. "You can't go in there. Fargo will kill you if he's still there."

He didn't stop or look back at Nan. If Fargo was waiting for him, he might do exactly what Nan had said, but maybe

Fargo would not be expecting him so soon. At least Clint hoped he wouldn't. Either way, he had to go after Danny.

He angled across the yard, slowing up now so Fargo wouldn't hear him. He drew his gun, stepped up on the porch and ducked under a window. Then he moved quickly through the door, his eyes sweeping the front room.

Doug Carney lay on one side of the table, his head beaten into a red mass of hair and brains and bone. Cousin Phil . . . he must be Duke Wade, Clint thought . . . lay on the other side, a bullet between his eyes. Neither Fargo nor the boy was in sight.

Clint plunged on into the kitchen. The room was empty. He looked in the pantry, and kicked open the door of Doug Carney's bedroom, then Nan's. Both rooms were empty. There was no upstairs. He wheeled to see Nan standing in the doorway staring at her father's body.

"Stay outside," he shouted. "I'll be back in a minute."

He ran out through the back door and looked in the woodshed, then the barn. A horse was there, but ordinarily neither Doug nor Nan kept a horse here. Doug never liked to ride, and Nan for the last year had left her horse in the livery stable.

Clint struck a match. The horse was a big bay gelding, an animal Clint had never seen before. He had been ridden hard, and the saddle was still on him. Clint left the barn and returned to the house. The bay was certainly the horse Fargo had ridden into San Lorenzo, probably stolen somewhere between here and Canon City.

When he stepped into the front room, he found Nan kneeling beside her father's body. He pulled her to her feet and led her outside. "You can't do anything for him now," he said. "I wish you hadn't seen him."

"So do I," she whispered. "Fargo hit him and kept on hitting him. He smashed Dad's head like you would a melon."

He made her sit down on the top step. ''Now tell me about it,'' he said.

She told him, haltingly, stopping now and then as a sob shook her whole body. When she was done, she said, ''Dad must have gone crazy. Why would he do these things? Have Duke Wade come and call him Cousin Phil and write on the barn door to scare everybody out of town and steal from his own bank? And then go up there and kill the Judge?''

Clint was silent a moment, knowing there was no adequate explanation he could give and that the truth about Doug Carney was almost as hard for Nan to accept as his death. Now Carney was dead because he had been foolish enough to think you could make a deal with a man like Ben Fargo. This was the kind of tragedy that could not be explained to Nan or understood by her. Only time would dull her pain.

''I don't know,'' he said. ''I suppose he brooded so much over the injuries he suffered from Wallace that he did go crazy.'' Clint took Nan's hands. They lay limp in his grasp as he went on, ''We'll have to think of it that way. Wallace was the kind of man who made people crazy. Like Fargo. Bonita isn't far from it.'' He thought briefly of his ranch that had been lost and his plans and dreams that had gone with it, and he added, ''We weren't free from Wallace's cussedness, Nan. If it hadn't been for him, we'd be married and have a kid or two by now.''

They were both reminded of Danny Tebo, and she asked, ''You think Fargo has killed Danny?''

''I don't think so. He's probably got a use for him or he'd have killed him here. Trouble is I don't have any idea where he's taken Danny.'' He considered a moment, then he said, ''Maybe he's got the idea he can use Danny to make me come after him. Did he say anything about what he aimed to do?''

''Yes. He was going to mark me up for you to see

before he killed you. Bogardus and Calloway weren't important. He'd kill them if he found them, but he wasn't going to waste time hunting for them. But the money was important. So were you and Wallace and Bonita.'' She paused as if trying to recall exactly what Fargo had said, but she was still suffering from shock. In a moment she added, ''He said I didn't mean anything to him but Danny did. He didn't say why or what he planned to do with Danny.''

Clint thought dismally there was no way he could determine how a mind like Fargo's would operate. Apparently it had been Doug Carney's admission that he had killed Wallace that had set Fargo off. Maybe he would go to Wallace's big house to see for himself whether Wallace was dead. If he could think of some way to locate Fargo; if he could find a means of negotiating for the boy's life . . .

Bonita! Fargo would not leave town without her. Perhaps in his warped way he loved her. Certainly he would not admit that she no longer loved him. He would probably expect to find her in the big house on the hill, but she was in the hotel. If he did not find her in Wallace's house, would he kill the boy in a wild outburst of disappointment? It was possible, even likely.

Bonita was the one bait that would lure Fargo into the open and possibly save Danny Tebo's life. Clint wasn't sure she would do what he wanted, or even sure he had a right to ask her, but he had to unless he could think of some other way to save Danny.

He rose and pulled Nan to her feet. ''We're going to the hotel to see Bonita. You'll be safer there than here.''

She obeyed without argument, moving silently beside him as if she were a sleepwalker.

TWENTY ONE

THE LOBBY WAS EMPTY WHEN CLINT AND NAN REACHED the hotel. The clerk, like nearly everyone else in town, had left. Clint climbed the stairs, Nan following. When he reached the landing, he saw that a door on down the hall was open, the lamplight falling on the faded carpet.

Clint drew his gun and ran toward the open door. He heard Bonita's voice, shrill and angry, and for one terrifying moment he was afraid that Fargo by sheer accident had stumbled into the girl's hiding place. But when he reached the door, he saw that it was Marge Rainer who was with Bonita.

He leaned against the casing the took a long breath. He said, ''Bonita, I told you to keep your door closed and locked.''

''Against Marge?'' Bonita shook her head. ''No, Clint. Never against her.''

Clint went into the room, glancing from Bonita to Marge and back to Bonita. He wondered what their argument had been about. Nan sat down on the bed. Marge looked at her, then sat down beside her, asking, "What happened, honey?"

"Fargo shot and killed Duke Wade," Nan said, "after he beat my father's brains out."

There was a moment of shocked silence, then Marge slipped an arm around Nan. "I'm sorry. We knew something like this would happen, but none of us dreamed it would be so bad." She looked at Clint. "He's got to be stalked and killed like an animal."

"Tell him, Marge," Bonita cried. "Damn it, tell him and let's get the job done."

"He's in my house, Clint," Marge said. "He's got Danny Tebo with him."

"The boy's all right?" Clint asked.

Marge nodded. "His face looked like he'd been cuffed a time or two and he's scared, but he's got a right to be."

"Why did he take Danny to your place?" Nan asked.

Marge looked at Bonita questioningly. Bonita said roughly, "Tell her that, too. It's all going to come out sometime."

"Bonita and Fargo wrote to each other for a while after he went to prison," Marge said. "The letters came to me, so I guess he thought I was the best go-between he could find. He asked if Bonita was in the Wallace house and I said I didn't think so, that she'd had a row with the Judge. Then he wanted to know where she was. I said I didn't know, so he told me I'd better find her and get her over there or the kid will get it."

Bonita looked at Clint. "That's what we were arguing about when you came in. Marge wanted to find you, and I said there wasn't time. I know what he's like when he's mad. He's probably worse now."

"What did you intend to do?" Clint asked.

"Go to him while Marge was hunting you. I thought I could do something for the boy, get Fargo to turn him loose. I'm not sure what I can do. Maybe nothing, but I am sure he'll kill the kid if I don't come."

"All right," Clint said. "You'd better go. Play up to him as if you were glad to see him. I'll be in front of the house. When you come out, I'll drill him."

"It won't work," Marge cried. "He told me he wouldn't leave town until he had killed you, Clint. He says he'll find you sooner or later and he'll keep the boy with him till he does."

"If Bonita . . ."

"Fargo's using Danny for all he's worth," Marge interrupted. "That's why I didn't want Bonita to go. I think he aims to kill the boy anyway, but before he does, he'll use him to get at you, Clint. Bonita, too. She's just throwing her life away."

"It doesn't make any difference," Bonita said tonelessly.

"You're wrong." Clint was silent a moment, then he added reluctantly, "We've got to try, Marge. Listen, Bonita. He'll need two horses if you go with him, so he'll have to go to the livery stable. I'll have Shorty to help. We'll get Fargo somewhere between Marge's house and the stable."

"All right," Bonita said, "but give me plenty of time. Don't rush us."

Clint nodded. "We'd better get at it."

"Don't do it," Marge said desperately. "This is wrong, Clint."

Clint glanced at Nan and saw that she was looking at him. They were both thinking of Danny, he knew, and how much better off he would have been if they had left him at home.

Clint and Bonita went down the stairs together. He looked at her as they crossed the lobby; he saw the strained, white expression of her face and he realized how thoroughly frightened she was. He said, "Play it easy and careful."

She tried to smile. "You never play easy and careful with Ben Fargo," she said, and disappeared into the darkness along the side of the hotel.

Clint hurried along the walk to the livery stable. He found Shorty Bogardus waiting in the archway. "Fargo's in Marge's house," Clint said. "Bonita's going in. He sent for her. We'll get him as he comes out. Get your shotgun and take the back door. I'll take the front door. You've got to be careful because he's got Danny Tebo and he'll have Bonita. He'll probably use both of them as hostages, so you'll have to try to get the drop on him somehow."

Shorty nodded, white-faced, but not backing up from the job Clint was giving him. "I'll do my damnedest."

"He'll come to the stable for horses. He left his in the Carney barn . . ."

"Clint."

He had been standing in the doorway, the light from the lantern overhead falling around him in a wide cone. He whirled to see Marge running toward him from the hotel. He waited, wasting precious seconds that should be used in getting around to the front of her house.

She was panting when she reached him. She put her hands on his arms. "Bonita's throwing her life away and you're letting her do it. She can't do any good. Fargo doesn't want her to go with him. He wants to kill her. She didn't want you to know what was in his last letters. She's so ashamed of writing to Fargo. He threatened her. He said no woman was going to throw him overboard like she did. He's kill crazy, Clint. She thinks she can sweet-talk him out of it, but . . .'"

Clint didn't wait to hear any more. He should never have let Bonita go. He should have known.

He ran the length of the runway and out through the

back door. He didn't know where Shorty was. More danger, he thought. Shorty might let go with the shotgun if he heard someone running. Clint saw the glow of lamplight ahead of him in Marge's house. Bonita would be there by this time.

He stumbled and recovered his footing and went on. He heard Fargo's angry voice cursing the girl. Then he was at the back door and his hand was on the knob turning it. The outlaw's words came to him clearly: "You married the Judge, then you wrote to me and said you still loved me, but you got to thinking about all that money, so I wasn't good enough for you. Well, before I leave this town, I'll have money, plenty of it."

Clint had slowly and silently turned the knob, but the door didn't open. Apparently Fargo had slammed the bolt home on the inside. Clint backed off, his gun in his hand, and drove forward, his shoulder smashing the door open. Fargo was standing in front of Bonita, his gun pointed at her. Danny wasn't in sight.

Clint fired point blank, but he was a fraction of a second too late. At the first sound of the door being broken open, Fargo had pulled the trigger. Bonita was slammed back against the wall by the impact of the slug. Her feet went out from under her and she fell.

Fargo wheeled to shoot Clint, but he never got off a second shot. Clint's first bullet caught him in the side, the next in the chest. He fired again as the man was falling. He knew the last shot was unnecessary, but he couldn't help it. He was driven by a hatred he had never known for another human being.

Holstering his gun, he ran to Bonita, yelling over his shoulder at Shorty Bogardus who had just come in, "Get Doc Julian. He's at Delong's place." He picked the girl up and carried her into Marge's bedroom. She had been hit in the chest, but it was off center and to the right, and so had missed the heart.

He laid her on the bed. Then Marge and Nan arrived, and he backed away, tears running down his cheeks for the first time since he had been a boy. Bonita had known what she was heading into, yet she had insisted on doing it in the slight hope she might save Danny Tebo.

Clint found the boy in the front room on the floor. Fargo had knocked him cold, probably to keep him out of the way and be sure he wouldn't run off. He wasn't badly hurt. Clint carried him home and put him to bed. He came around then, and Clint told him that Fargo was dead.

As long as Clint lived, he would never forget the painful smile that came to the boy's lips as he said, "I knew you'd get him, Clint. I knew you would."

Clint stayed until Mrs. Tebo returned. He said curtly, "Danny's all right," and left the house.

He had Shorty hitch up a wagon and help him move the bodies to Doc Julian's place. It was close to morning before they finished. The doctor had returned and was stomping around and growling that San Lorenzo didn't need a hospital but it sure needed a bigger morgue.

"Bonita?" Clint asked.

"She'll make it with good nursing," Julian said, "and she's sure going to get that from Marge. She's conscious and she wants to see you."

Dawn was reaching across the sky when Clint went again to Marge's house. Nearly twenty-four hours had passed from the time he had knocked on Marge's door yesterday morning to get Tom Ludlow. The hour hand of the clock had gone full circle twice, and in that time dreams and hopes had been destroyed, people had shown what they were when the veneer of safe living in a law-and-order society was peeled from them, and death had been busy.

From now on life in San Lorenzo would be different. People would be free from the fear of Ben Fargo's return and from the heavy hand of Judge Ezra Wallace. Clint could not say which would be the greatest relief. But of all the things that had happened, he thought that Bonita going to Fargo was the hardest to understand.

Nan let him in through the back door. She said, "She wants to see you. I don't know why."

Marge was sitting beside Bonita's bed. She rose when Clint came in and said, "He's here."

The girl seemed barely alive, Clint thought, as he stood looking down at her, her dark hair spread across the pillow. She lifted a hand and he took it in his. She whispered, "I'm a fairy. I'll grant you any wish you want. What is it?"

"A loan from the bank," he said. "I want my old ranch back."

"I'll speak to Mack Ferguson," she said. "The sky's the limit."

"Thanks," he said.

"No thanks to me," she said. "They're all from me to you."

Marge shooed him out and he said he'd look in later in the day. Nan left with him. When they were outside, he asked, "Why did she do it? Or why didn't she tell me the truth in the hotel room before she left?"

"I'm not sure," Nan said. "I talked to Marge about it. Marge thinks she wanted to die because she blamed herself for all this, writing to Fargo and telling him she still loved him after she married the Judge. But I have another idea. I think she had a notion she could bargain for Danny's life."

"I'd rather believe that." He took Nan's hand as they walked through the gathering dawn light, then he added, "I guess the sun's going to make it this morning after all."

She smiled. "You know something, Clint? I knew it would."